Bobbin for Answers

A HARLOW CASSIDY MAGICAL DRESSMAKING MYSTERY

MELISSA BOURBON

Lake House
Press

Also Available in the Harlow Cassidy Magical Dressmaking Mysteries

Pleating for Mercy
A Fitting End
Deadly Patterns
A Killing Notion
A Custom-Fit Crime
A Seamless Murder
Bobbin for Answers
Bodice of Evidence

*Praise for the Harlow Cassidy
Magical Dressmaking Mysteries*

TOP PICK

"A charming, whimsical tale that's also chock full of sex, lies, intrigue, and murder...one heckuva series debut. Harlow is a marvelous heroine. Smart, funny, and full of fire. Bourbon's supporting cast is remarkable, as well – a perfect blend of quirk, menace, and heart...the image-conscious, richer-than-God Kincaid family could have been plucked straight from an episode of Dallas; and hunky architect-slash-handyman Will Flores and his young daughter Gracie add heat and warmth (respectively) to the story.

Run to your nearest bookstore and snap up a copy of this whimsical take on a supernatural cozy; you just may find me there standing in line to buy the sequel." **~ The Season for Romance**

"This series debut by Bourbon (who also writes the "Lola Cruz" series under the name Misa Ramirez) has a clever premise, lots of interesting trade secrets, snappy dialog, and the requisite quirky and lovable family. It's very Texas, and

Wendy Lyn Watson fans should enjoy. A fun read with plenty of potential.." ~ **Library Journal**

"A crime-solving ghost and magical charms...a sure winner!" ~ **NY Times Bestselling Author Maggie Sefton**

"A seamless blend of mystery, magic, and dress-making, with a cast of masterfully tailored characters you'll want to visit again and again." ~ **NY Times Bestselling Author, Jennie Bentley**

"Enchanting! Prepare to be spellbound from page one by this well-written and deftly-plotted cozy. It's charming, clever and completely captivating! Fantasy, fashion and a foul play—all sewn together by a wise and witty heroine you'll instantly want as a best friend. Loved it!" ~ **Hank Phillippi Ryan Agatha, Anthony and Macavity winning author**

"Cozy couture! Harlow Jane Cassidy is a tailor-made amateur sleuth. Bourbon stitches together a seamless mystery, adorned with magic, whimsy, and small-town Texas charm." ~ **Wendy Lyn Watson, Author of NAL's Mystery a la Mode series**

"I was really happy and satisfied when I was finished with "Pleating for Mercy" and I want more cozy mysteries like this one." ~ **About Happy Books**

"This is a fun read, perfect for vacation or, if you're like me, holed up on your bed turning the pages at 2 AM to find out what happens. I'm looking forward to the next installment in this new series." ~ **Stitches and Seams**

"How can you not like a character that can drink a hot cup of Joe as easily on a sweltering day as she can on a chilly 40-degree one and calls herself a "Project Runway," "Dancing with the Stars" and "Iron Chef" kinda gal." **~ AnnArbor.com**

"Pleating for mercy is an engaging novel! It kept me up late, wanting to know how all the details worked out in the end, and making sure my favorite characters were as friendly as I had imagined. I loved how fabric was woven into each part of the story, as the characters weave their own tale." **~ Amy's Creative Side**

"This is the first book in a blissfully enchanting and entertaining series that I hope is here to stay." **~ Notes from Me**

"Harlow is a clever, down-to-earth main character who you can't help but like. Most of the action takes place right in her dress shop, and Harlow asks all the right questions as she tries to figure out the murder mystery....Fans of cozy mysteries will want to be sure to put this one at the top of their "to be read" list." **~ Two Lips Reviews**

"What can I say about this debut series? "Charm"(ing), intriguing, and satisfying; a page-turner with the right touch of potential romance and paranormal just about covers it." **~ Once Upon a Romance**

"This book was a fun read, and the historical tie-in with Butch Cassidy was a kick, as well." **~ Fresh Fiction**

"PLEATING FOR MERCY is a fantastic first book in a new cozy mystery series by Melissa Bourbon. I was quickly absorbed in the book and did not want to put it down!" **~ Book of Secrets**

"This opening act in the new paranormal amateur sleuth A

Dressmaker's Mystery is as enchanting as the magic of the Cassidy women is a two edged sword of both a blessing and a curse. Pleating for Mercy is a spirited whodunit." **~ The Mystery Gazette**

"Harlow is such an interesting character.I enjoyed this book a lot and felt it was a great first book in a series and sets readers up well for what's to come.Using comic relief to lighten the mood is a common tool employed in cozy mysteries, but I think this one takes it to a new height." **~ Deb's Book Bag**

"Filled with twists, turns, laughs and mystery, this is a MUST read for that rainy night, that lazy fall day by the fire, or just any time you are looking for a warm, suspenseful, fun read by a wonderful author!" **~ Reviews by Molly**

"This is the first in A Magical Dressmaking Mystery series, and it is a charming debut. It's full of Texas small town flavor, unique and interesting characters (Grandma the goat whisperer? I love it), good plotting and just enough romance." ~ **Over My Dead Body**

"The book is a blissful read, is suitable for ages preteen, and up, and would make a nice back to school gift for a student or a teacher-but don't forget to buy an extra copy for yourself!" ~ **Myshelf**

"A highly enjoyable paranormal cozy mystery! It would be highly enjoyable no matter the genre label." **~Vixen Books**

"...a good one." **~ Storybook Reviews**

"Talented Harlow Cassidy, descendent of Butch, helps clear a high school football player who's falsely accused of murder in

this light paranormal Texas cozy. The series stands at five (after A Custom-Fit Crime); sewing tips and recipes included."
~*Library Journal*, **April 2014**

4 stars, RT Book Reviews
"Harlow is back and ready to dig into another murder. Bourbon has done a great job with the plot and characters, and the mystery surrounding the murder is fascinating. Readers will find themselves trying to guess what happens, but will end up shocked at the conclusion. With each series installment, Bourbon gets better." *~RT Book Reviews*

4 STARS "This enchanting mystery with down-home charm is as comfortable as slipping into your favorite dress and sitting down and drinking sweet tea with engaging characters who quickly become old friends." ~ The Mystery Reader

"The magic, the mystery, the small town cozy feel, and the nicely balanced mix of characters of all ages make this book a read that promises to entertain those of various generations. It would be a wonderful selection for a mother/daughter book group, a sewing group who likes to read as well, and for those will just plain love the cozy mystery genre...The twist at the end was like the cherry on top of a swirly delicious ice cream on a hot day." ~Laura Hinds

Published by Lake House Press, USA

Cover Design by Mariah Sinclair | www.mariahsinclair.com

ISBN: 9798863899039

For every Wednesday Addams fan and every lover of Halloween.

And to Carole Pickett for inspiring the Harlow Cassidy Family song.

The Cassidy Family Theme Song

(snap, snap)

They're charming and they're kooky,
Meemaw's getting spooky.
The murders are kinda ooky,
That's Harlow's family.

Her charms, you will believe 'em,
A wish sewn into each se'am.
Meemaw makes 'em scre'am,
That's Harlow's family.

[snap twice]
(Neat)
[snap twice]
(Sweet)
[snap twice]
[snap twice]
(Neat)
[snap twice]

(Petite)
[snap twice]

So come and try your dress on,
Magic's sewn into each o-ne,
Your wishes, you will get 'em,
That's Harlow's family!

(snap, snap)

Inspired by the Addams Family Theme Song

Chapter One

You might think the great-great-great granddaughter of Butch Cassidy would fall on the wrong side of justice. After all, Butch and his Hole-in-the-Wall Gang did their fair share of dark deeds during their reign as bandits in the West. But the three most important women in my life—Tessa Cassidy, Coleta Cassidy, and Loretta Mae Cassidy—had taught me right from wrong. There wasn't much gray when it came to their moral compasses.

And although I'd had some run-ins with Hoss McClaine during my rebellious teenage years—and more recently with his deputy son, Gavin—I was basically a rule-follower. Case in point, when I caught a coworker rifling through my friend Orphie Cates's sewing station in the Maximilian workroom during my stint as a New York fashion designer, there was no way I wasn't going to call her out on it.

The workroom was divided into sections just like in Project Runway. Maximilian's minions (that's what we called ourselves because we were the worker bees that made his designs come to life) had their own stations, each with a large cutting table, a dress form, a sewing machine, and a serger.

That day, I'd come to work early so expected the workroom to be blissfully quiet—and it was. But it wasn't empty. I saw a figure hunched over Orphie's notions box the second I entered the vast room. I knew for a fact that it wasn't, in fact, Orphie because Orphie and I were roommates in a shoebox loft a few blocks from the garment district and she had just been rolling out of bed when I left.

I zigzagged through the room, my rubber-soled boots silent on the linoleum floor. The culprit stood and I froze, thinking she'd heard me, but then she crouched in front of the set of plastic drawers next to Orphie's sewing machine. The intruder slid the bottom drawer out, where I knew Orphie kept one of her sketchbooks, a stack of fashion magazines, and a collection of Maximilian LookBooks. I walked up right behind the interloper before jamming my hands on my hips and clearing my throat.

Loudly.

The woman screeched and stumbled back, landing on her backside. Busted.

She turned and I gasped. The thief wasn't just any coworker. It was Juletta Sandberg—a woman, until this moment in time, I'd called a friend.

Seeing her with Orphie's sketchbook in her hot little hands made it clear that Juletta Sandberg did *not* have the moral compass I did. "What do you think you're doing?" I demanded.

Not that I'd needed to ask. She'd been trying to steal Orphie's designs to pass them off as her own. Instead, I'd caught her red-handed and the shift supervisor had cut her loose then and there.

Little did I know that Orphie's moral compass had a lot of gray in it and that she'd done something very similar to what Juletta had attempted—only with Maximilian.

Orphie had shown up one day on my porch with one of

Maximilian's design books tucked away in her suitcase. Her moral compass had skewed in the wrong direction, and that had tested my sense of justice, but she'd come to me for help in making it right.

Lucky for her, her beau, who was my new step-brother Gavin McClaine, and I had saved her from herself. She'd mailed back the stolen LookBook, and all was right in the world.

I hadn't thought of that incident—or Juletta—in years. Orphie? Yes. Since inexplicably falling for Gavin, she'd been spending her time right here in Bliss. But at this moment, with the infuriating sound of the woodpecker who'd been jackhammering against the side of the house, tormenting me with the echoing sound in my brain, it wasn't Orphie on the porch of Buttons & Bows, my little dressmaking shop. It was the woman who'd tried to steal her designs all those years ago. I stared, slack-jawed. My chin dipped and my glasses slipped down. I shoved them back up, scanning the woman standing before me. Short black hair sticking out and up from her head all topsy-turvy. A shapeless dress. Chunky wedge heels. "Juletta?"

"Harlow," she said. Her face was pale, her lips even more so.

"What are you doing here?" I asked, my parallel question being, how had she even found me?

In response, she held up a copy of Dallas Magazine, which had recently done an article on several local designers, including me. I wasn't sure it had garnered me any new business, but it was hard to say. I couldn't always grill a new customer, asking where they'd heard of me. Anyway, the truth of the matter was that nine times out of ten, they'd been referred by Zinnia James, my benefactor and biggest fan.

What I hadn't expected from the article was that it would bring someone from my past straight into my present. The biting October air—unseasonably cold for my little bucolic sliver of Texas—was pushing up against the warmer air inside. Meemaw had drilled the idea of bought air into me. "I pay good money for this bought air, so you might could help me keep the bill down by closin' that door and not lettin' it all fly right out," she used to say.

Now that I was paying the bills for the bought air, I understood. Meemaw had gifted me her old yellow farmhouse with the redbrick accents on the day I was born. No one knew why, and no one ever would. I'd only learned about it after she passed. Now, here I was, a former Maximilian minion, staring right into the eyes of another, the chill from outside hitting the wall of the heat inside. I opened the door a little more and ushered Juletta inside.

At the last second, I poked my head out and shooed away the woodpecker. The pounding of its beak stopped, but the pounding in my head kept right on going as I turned to face Juletta. The woman now standing in front of me did not look like the one I'd known a few years ago. That woman had carried herself with a strong air of self-assurance. She had worn her hair in an artfully coiffed style that looked breezy and effortless. Now, she looked like a disheveled version of her old self, the hair not so carefully arranged, her demeanor less than it used to be.

When I'd known her, *she'd* worn her clothes, but now it looked like her clothes wore her. Her black cotton dress was oversized and hung limply on her thin frame. She sank down onto the red velvet settee in my showroom, which was really just the farmhouse's living room. She crossed one leg over the other, the top foot shaking nervously.

The coffee table was an old door I'd repurposed. Buttons & Bows was Project Runway—the old one with Heidi and Tim—with a small-town Southern flair. My designs often had a hint of something that reflected that part of myself. I just couldn't help it. You can take the girl out of Texas, but you can't take Texas out of the girl.

The house itself at 2112 Mockingbird Lane sat off the square but the property backed up to my grandmother's. The unique and sometimes offensive smell of her goat herd— Sundance Kids—sometimes wafted through my open windows and Thelma Louise, the herd queen, was often in my yard eating my flowers or pressing her nose up against a window. She should have been named Houdini, what with her ability to escape Nana's fencing.

I perched on the edge of the coffee table, facing Juletta. "What are you doing here?"

Before she could answer, a groan came from deep inside the walls of the house, a low and sonorous sound like a foghorn bellowing. Juletta's head snapped up and her eyes went wide. "What was that?"

That was Loretta Mae making her presence known. My ghostly great-grandmother hadn't gone away when she'd passed. No, as it was for all the Cassidy women—an unintended result of Butch's wish in a magical Argentinian fountain eons ago, which had enchanted all the Cassidy women in his line—dead didn't mean gone. Meemaw haunted me and this house. Not in a spooky, scary, run-for-your-life kind of way, but just in an ever-present fashion.

"Old pipes," I said dismissively because it was easier that way. Only a handful of people actually knew about our magical gifts. Mama with her green thumb. Nana with her goat-whispering. Me with my ability to sew a person's wishes and dreams into a garment. Gracie Flores with her power to see the past of a garment, in all its glorious history. When *her* gift had first materialized, the images had bombarded her like bullets, jarring her to the point of withdrawal. No one had known about her connection to Butch Cassidy. We'd always thought Texana Harlow, who I was named after, was his true

5

love. He'd left her pregnant when he'd escaped to Argentina but as it turns out, he'd also left Etta Place in the family way; Gracie's mother was a descendent from *that* line. And then there were Sandra and Libby Allen, also descendants of Etta Place and Butch Cassidy.

Oh, Butch. What a tangled genetic web he'd woven. When he'd wished that his female descendants lived charmed lives, that meant *all* his female descendants, not just those through Texana's lineage.

The lowing sound came again and Juletta blinked, her eyes opening wide. "That does not sound like any pipes I've ever heard."

All I could do was shrug because she was right. I turned my back to her. "Meemaw!" I whispered harshly, just quiet enough that Juletta couldn't hear me.

The house moaned again and then fell silent. I muttered to myself. Oh, that ghost of a woman. She was going to expose us all one of these days.

Chapter Two

Before I'd known Juletta would be showing up on my doorstep, I'd offered to help Josie Kincaid, née Sandoval, set up for the Halloween party she and her husband Nate were hosting. Nate came from a well-to-do family, but there had been some drama recently that had taken the family down a notch or two. Thankfully Nate had not been involved. He had Josie to keep him grounded, and they had their six-month-old little girl, Molly.

Nate grew up in a sprawling house Gracie Flores, my future stepdaughter, had called The Castle. It had an arched stone bridge, a pond, a waterway that was reminiscent of a moat, and an enormous house with vaulted ceilings and fancy chandeliers. The party I'd attended there with Madelyn Brighton, the town's official photographer and unofficial ghost-hunter, had been a veritable who's who of the Texas elite. The men had worn Texas tuxedos—classic blazers with dark jeans, big silver belt buckles, and cowboy boots; the women's hands and necks were laden with diamonds, and cleavage—real and otherwise—was on ample display.

Josie and Nate's Halloween party was going to be the

polar opposite of *that* ostentatious display. They lived in an old firehouse they'd converted into a home. It had charm and originality that no new build ever could. It fit Josie to a T.

"Bring her along," Josie said over the phone when I told her an old friend—a word I used lightly—had shown up. Frenemy was more accurate, but I decided not to go into the down-and-dirty details. I hadn't yet told Orphie that Juletta had shown up on my doorstep. Of course, I'd never told her that Juletta had tried to steal her designs, so she wouldn't harbor any ill will. With them both in the same room, I just hoped I could keep what I knew about both of them under wraps. I tended to wear my emotions on my sleeve.

"A Halloween party," Juletta said dryly, her old self reemerging. She spoke as if that particular type of celebration was beneath her.

"Um, you tried to steal from my friend. I think you can manage stringing fake cobwebs for a Halloween party," I said, realizing, of course, that one thing had absolutely nothing to do with the other. If Juletta had made the non-connection, she didn't say. She just frowned.

"Is it a kid party?" she asked from the passenger side of Buttercup, the old yellow pickup truck I'd inherited from Meemaw, right along with the yellow farmhouse. Yellow had been my great-great-grandmother's favorite color. Even the retro appliances in the kitchen sparkled like the sun.

I tucked my hair behind my ears. "Their baby is…a baby… so, no, it's not a kid party."

"A grown-up Halloween party. How…droll."

The way she said it was laced with judgment. It was the type of thing Lori Kincaid, Nate's mother, said, not something that came out of the mouths of people in my circle. I used my index finger to push my black-framed glasses up the bridge of my nose as I leveled my gaze at her. "Looks to me like you could stand for a little drollness in your life," I said.

"Rude," she'd snapped.

I balked. "Juletta, *you* showed up at *my* house and you haven't told me anything. So...again...why are you here?"

She harrumphed and started to tell me something, but then zipped her lips closed. No amount of questions got her to open up. She scraped her fingers through her spiky hair, making it stand on end even more than it had been before. All of her bravado dissolved into thin air leaving a more vulnerable Juletta behind. "I just...I can't...give me some time, Harlow, okay?"

One thing I didn't have a lot of was time. On my list of Things to Do were finishing Gracie and Libby's costumes, as well as my own. But I'd promised Josie I'd help her decorate, and I couldn't back out now. Argh. My head hurt.

"Take your time," I told Juletta, but inside I silently urged her to spit it out so we could move on.

She didn't.

I glanced at her, then did a double-take when I saw how pale she'd turned. How blue her lips were. "Hey, are you okay?"

She pressed one hand to her chest and looked out the window. Her chest rose and fell as she drew in a deep inhalation, and then blew it out. I slowed down, looking over my shoulder so I could change lanes. "Juletta? Should I pull over?"

She let out another loud breath as she turned forward again. "No. I'm fine. It just...it happens sometimes. I just get dizzy and—"

"I thought you were going to faint," I said, putting my foot back on the gas pedal.

"Breathing helps," she said, then she jammed her lips together. It was clear she didn't want to talk about it so I let it go.

Buttercup bounced along and soon I pulled up to Josie

and Nate's old firehouse home. Several cars lined the street in front of it and I could see the hustle and bustle of worker bees spooky-ing up the place. I did a three-point turn and parked my truck on the opposite side of the street. As Juletta and I crossed back to Josie's house, I admired it. She and Nate had remodeled it during the first year of their marriage and while she was pregnant with Molly. Now it was a showcase with a large porch, wood floors, built-in bookshelves, exposed beams, and wide moldings around the windows and doors.

Like all good Southern homes, the porch they'd added held several rocking chairs, which were currently stacked with boxes and bags of spooky decorations. An old barrel was in the back corner, and orange lights hung along the awnings Nate had added to the brick facade. Josie was going all out.

Juletta trailed behind me as I walked up the steps and smack into a wispy cottony string of cobwebs. I stopped short. Sputtered. Because fake cobwebs caught in your mouth were almost as unpleasant as the real thing.

Juletta plowed into my back, shoving me forward and into another tangled mass.

As I picked the strands of finely spun cotton from my mouth and hair, Juletta shrieked and flapped her hands in the air. "Ew ew ew! Get it off me!"

The webs had snagged her, too.

She clawed at her face and hair as if the actual sticky gossamer of a real spider's web stuck to her rather than the manufactured threads that had come from a plastic bag.

I stifled a laugh as I dragged my fingers through my hair, freeing the last of the webbing. "You okay there?"

She glared at me as she swatted at the flying wisps of polyester still clinging to her. "Just peachy," she snarked, and then she muttered something under her breath.

The sound of giggling came from the back corner of the porch. Giggling I recognized. "Gracie?"

The old oak barrel rocked and three figures rose from behind them, looking like Jack-in-the-Boxes popping up in slow motion. My future stepdaughter and my sewing assistant, Gracie Flores, her cousin, Libby Allen, and their friend Holly Kincaid covered their mouths with open palms, trying to hold in their laughter. "That was hilarious!" Holly guffawed.

Libby hitched at the waist, giggling and Gracie sang out, "Trick or treat!"

A low guttural sound came from Juletta. "That is not funny," she snapped. "Somebody might have a real fear of spiders."

Their faces fell, the wind snatched from their sails. Gracie flung a look at us, then at Holly and Libby. She waved one hand in apology. "Josie said to put them up...we didn't mean to—"

"It's fine," I said, waving away Juletta's bad manners. "All good. They're not real cobwebs, so no harm done." I backhanded Juletta's arm. "Right?"

She just grumbled, still plucking at invisible strands she felt clinging to her face.

"Juletta," I said with a hiss. "It's Halloween. They're decorations."

She pulled a face then shouldered past me and threw open the front door, letting herself into the house of a woman she didn't even know.

I glanced at the girls. They'd all turned pale and Holly's mouth was in an O. "Ignore her," I said. "The decorations are great."

They nodded, like puppets whose strings were being pulled at the same time. I gave them another encouraging smile, looked at the webs strung across the porch with approval, and scooted into the house.

In the living room, more cobwebs were strung in wispy lengths from lampshades to plantation blinds to the corners of furniture. I was sure Josie would screw in a blue lightbulb to cast gloom into the room during the party, but at the moment light streamed through the side windows, bathing the space with a bright glow.

I followed the sound of voices and laughter into the kitchen, stopping short at the sight before me. Portable tables were lined up and covered with plastic tablecloths. Cookies in different Halloween shapes were spread across one of the tables. Another held white pumpkins in varying states of decoration. Some were stenciled with witches in flight, others with skeletons, and still others with spooky trees, branches sharply angled and reaching around the gourds. Off to one side was a large glass punchbowl turned upside down. Underneath was a stack of green skulls. A bowl of red apples sat on the counter. It was Halloween central.

A crew of women milled around the house. Josie surged forward when she saw me, Molly in her arms, one of her little fists clutching a handful of Josie's hair. "Oh thank God you're here," Josie said in a rush. "There's too much to do. What was I thinking?"

"The place looks amazing!" I gushed. It really did.

Josie glanced around. "Do you think so? It's such a mess and the party is tomorrow!" She thrust a sheet of paper at me. "Look at my To Do list! Even with all this help, I don't know how I can get it all done."

Josie and I were similar in our organizational methods. We both loved our lists. I scanned hers.

Decorate cookies
Finish pumpkins
String orange lights and cobwebs
Nate-set up speakers and spooky playlist
Finish costume
Halloween photos of Molly
Appetizers!
Appetizer table!
Set up bobbing for apple barrel

It went on and on and on. "It *is* a lot," I said. I gestured to the women scurrying around. "But you have all this help. And the orange lights and cobwebs are done."

She snatched the list back and used an orange Flair pen to cross those particular tasks off the list.

I put my hands on my hips and looked around. "Now tell me, what can I do?"

Josie's eyes strayed over my shoulder. I turned and saw Juletta lurking there like she was up to something. I eyed her suspiciously. "This is Juletta," I told Josie. "We worked together at Maximillian. She, uh, surprised me with a visit last night."

"Gorgeous house," Juletta said. I thought I sensed sincerity in her voice but I wasn't entirely convinced.

The cheeks of Josie's lovely brown skin tinted pink with the compliment. "Aw, thank you. Turning a firehouse into a *house* house takes a lot of time. Definitely a labor of love."

"It shows."

"What brings you to Bliss?" Josie asked, cutting to the

chase. She was not one to mince words, and at the moment, she didn't have time even if she wanted to pour a glass of sweet tea and settle in for a story.

Juletta forced a smile. "Just passing through and thought I'd stop by to see Harlow. It's been a while."

Lies, lies, lies. I still didn't know why she'd come, but it wasn't happenstance.

Josie hiked Molly higher on her hip. With her free hand, she reached for mine and squeezed. "Harlow is one of my oldest friends. We were in elementary school together, can you believe that? And now I'm married and a mother and she's engaged."

"You are?" Juletta asked, clearly surprised.

"I am," I said.

Gracie, Libby, and Holly blew into the house, teenage balls of energy. The encounter with the cobwebs had clearly flitted out of their minds. "She is!" Gracie exclaimed, inserting herself into the conversation. "She's engaged to my dad."

Juletta swung her gaze to my left hand and blinked. I held it up so she could see the ring—a family heirloom—Meemaw had led Will to. "Wow," she said. "That looks...old."

I got the feeling that wasn't a compliment, but I pretended it was. "My great-great-great-granddaddy gave it to my great-great-great-grandmother before he, uh, went away on a trip."

"Wait a sec." Understanding crossed Juletta's face. "I remember that story. Not about the ring, but your...however many greats grandfather. He was Butch Cassidy, right? Like, the real one, not Paul Newman. Too bad. I bet Paul Newman was better looking than the real thing."

I shrugged. It *was* hard to beat Paul Newman—or Robert Redford for that matter—in the looks department. Those two were in a league of their own. My ancestor Butch Cassidy didn't have the piercing blue eyes that Paul Newman had, but he hadn't needed them to get the girls. Everyone loves a bad guy, it seemed. Everyone but me. Given the choice between an outlaw and a good guy, I'd take the good guy any day of the week. I'd found my own tall drink of water in Will Flores.

Molly lurched, propelling herself toward Holly. She gurgled and wriggled, reaching for her cousin with outstretched arms. "Do you mind?" Josie asked.

Holly made goo-goo noises back at Molly. "Nope," she said. Josie handed her over, and then Holly, Libby, and Gracie scurried off with the six-month-old.

We followed Josie around as she showed us what party preparations she'd already done and what still needed to be checked off the list. She opened the French doors from the dining room that led to the side of the add-on porch. "The apple bobbing'll be out here," she said. "It's really for show. All that shared spit and germs? Yuk. But Holly really wanted it, and you know when a teenager wants something, it's hard to say no. So there you go. Bobbing for apples."

"It's a kid party, too?" Juletta asked, sending me a pointed look as if I'd intentionally lied to her.

"Teens and adults. Other than Molly, no little ones." She chuckled. "We'll have plenty of years ahead of us for *that* kind of party."

The idea of children's parties danced in my head like sugarplums. Or maybe candy corn. Will had Gracie, and now I did, too. Did we want to grow our family beyond the three of us? That remained to be seen. The wedding had to come first, and we hadn't done one iota of planning. We'd barely gotten through Mama's wedding to Sheriff Hoss McClaine intact. Actually, we hadn't even succeeded at that. Tessa had been a no-show, Hoss had gone after her, and before a cowboy could say giddy-up, they'd done and gotten hitched without all the fanfare we'd spent months planning.

One thing at a time. I reckoned we could get through the holidays and then we'd see what was what.

Josie and her friends—including me and Juletta—worked for two straight hours. Finally, we all collapsed into chairs in the kitchen. A few of the women wielded bags of icing and were decorating the cookies. "That's a lot of ghosts and witches," Juletta murmured.

"Check it off," I said to Josie. She did, but then she scribbled two more things at the bottom of the list.

My lists were like that, too. Two steps forward, one step back. Before I could see what else Josie had added, the front door blew open with a bang. A young woman in her twenties walked in, her arm threaded through the arm of an older woman with olive skin sagging from age, hunched shoulders, a slack jaw, and cloudy eyes. She shuffled forward, using a cane to help her.

"*Abuela*!" Josie exclaimed, rushing forward. Josie grasped her grandmother's hands, then moved closer for a hug.

I stared, stunned at how Yolanda Sandoval had aged since I'd seen her last. "Thank you, Abby," Josie said to the young woman who'd stepped aside.

"Of course," Abby said with a smile.

"Is she having a good day?" Josie asked.

"We're here!" Abby answered, and then she looked at Josie's grandmother. "Yolanda? It's been a good day, hasn't it?"

Yolanda Sandoval lifted her cloudy eyes to Abby, then to Josie. She dipped her chin the tiniest bit and her lips quivered as she tried to smile. "Come on, *Abuela*." Josie guided her grandmother to the kitchen chair, easing her down. Yolanda propped her cane between her knees, leaning heavily on it for support. Josie sat next to her grandmother. She gave a concerned look to the young woman, Abby, who nodded her understanding—it wasn't a good day for Yolanda—then forced a watery smile. "I'm so glad you're here, *Abuela*."

Chapter Three

While Yolanda sat quietly at the table, the women in Josie's kitchen had a good old-fashioned Southern chinwag as they finished decorating cookies and carving pumpkins. The energy in the room sizzled with their excitement. A Halloween party for grown-ups!

Josie went around the room, introducing everyone for Juletta's sake. She started with Jacklyn Padeski, who stood bone-thin and eagle-eyed and stood about five feet five inches. "Jaclyn lives next door," she said.

I'd met Jaclyn once or twice, and seen her several times when I'd visited my hairdresser at Salon 63 where she had a space of her own. Truth be told, I always felt as if I was being scrutinized in her company. She and Josie weren't besties, but Josie would never *not* invite a neighbor to a party she was having. "Because my mama and *Abuela* raised me that way," Josie had said when Nate asked her why she was inviting Jaclyn. Which was true. "You do not have to be rich to treat people right," I'd heard her say more than once. Both Mrs. Sandovals had been forces to be reckoned. Josie's mom still was, but age had taken Yolanda's fire. Loretta Mae, Nana, and

Mama had taught me the very same life lesson. I smiled at Jaclyn, but a shiver ran through me at the way she tightened her mouth as she looked at Yolanda, as if she were an owl and Yolanda was a mouse. A bubble of something inexplicable bubbled up inside me, but I tamped it down. Age robbed the most vibrant people of their color. The moment I thought those words, an image of Mrs. Sandoval clashed in my mind. Orange and yellow and red, like a sunset. I didn't see more than that, but it was enough. Mrs. Sandoval needed color rather than the sand-colored clothing hanging limply on her body. After the party, I'd talk to Josie about designing a garment for her grandmother.

"And this is Abby Lassiter," Josie continued, pointing to the woman who'd brought Yolanda. She had her highlighted hair pulled into a high ponytail. Her jeans and cowboy boots were casual compared to the sparkling earrings and necklace she had on, but it worked. She wore her bling like any good Texan woman did. "I'm so glad we made it," Abby said, sending a quick smile at Mrs. Sandoval. "We might not stay long, though."

"Abby looks after my grandmother," Josie said.

"I'm a home health nurse," Abby said with a wave.

Josie reached for Abby's hand and gave it a heartfelt squeeze. "And a good one, and we're so thankful. We'd be lost without you," she said, then shook her head as if she wanted to dislodge whatever thoughts brewed there.

"Well I love it," Abby said, "and Yolanda is great."

Josie forced another small smile, but it grew as she moved on, wrapping her arm around Holly. "And this is my husband's niece—"

"Yours, too," Holly said, grinning at Josie.

Josie laughed. "Right. Mine, too. The perks of marriage. And I love you!" Next, she pointed to Gracie, then Libby. "And these are her besties. And that's Rowena Adams, who you've all probably seen at the library. She runs the circulation desk—"

"Among other things," Rowena said as she brushed her dark bangs from her eyes. "I'm a librarian." Her tone of voice sounded like she was issuing a challenge like we were going to gang up on her and say, *Do we really need librarians anymore?*

Which, of course, we did. Just as we needed writers and musicians and dressmakers. "And I'm Madison," a blonde-haired woman piped up. She had lips in the shape of a bow, eyes set close together, and pronounced cheekbones. She was unique. Striking, even. And based on the jumper she wore, she was clued into fashion trends. "I teach eleventh-grade history at the high school," she said.

So Gracie, Libby, and Holly might well be in her class when they got to their junior years. Most of the other women I recognized, and some I knew through Josie, but I didn't think there was any way Juletta would remember any of them. She proved me wrong right off the bat when she turned to Rowena and stared. "Adams, like the Addams Family?"

Rowena arched a brow and her lips twisted in a way that suggested she'd heard that question more than enough times in her life. "Sadly, yes. My parents were big fans. I'm lucky I was born on a Saturday instead of Wednesday."

"Yeah, lucky for you," Juletta said.

"That woulda been really cool, though," Holly said. She'd bounced Molly, who was now perched on her lap wringing her pudgy hands together and goo-goo'd her agreement. "Our own real-life Wednesday Addams."

With her long black hair hanging in a curtain down her back and her pale skin looking like it rarely saw the sun— which was a feat in Texas, where the sun blazed bright and hot across a big, open sky—she *did* fit the bill. Morticia would have been a far worse name, in my opinion, though. As it stood, Rowena was not bad at all.

The conversation drifted in different directions and Josie gave tasks to everyone, stopping to check in on Yolanda, who watched the women in the kitchen with a blank expression. It was hard to tell how much of what was happening was actually sinking in.

Some of the women continued painting small white pumpkins. Others kept decorating the abundance of Halloween cookies Josie had baked. I set to work with a needle and thread, fixing a hole in the tablecloth Josie had pushed into my arms. A steady hum filled the room as we all talked and worked, interrupted only when Jaclyn cleared her throat. She pursed her lips as she looked at each person in turn.

Josie bristled under the scrutiny of her neighbor's gaze. "What? What is it?"

Jaclyn dipped her chin and pushed out her lips. "I was just thinking..."

She trailed off without saying more. She was an odd duck, that was for sure, but Josie was a bloodhound. She wasn't about to drop it. The weight of Jaclyn 's stare had crawled under her skin. "About what?" she demanded.

Jaclyn 's lips quirked up on one side in a dark grin as if she'd known Josie would press. "Murder."

A hush fell over the room.

Josie's voice dropped low. Almost accusatory. "What do you mean, *murder*?"

"It's a good topic for the holiday next week, don't you think...and for the party tomorrow?" She thrust her arms out like Frankenstein and wriggled her fingers. "Mwahaha."

Josie bristled and I thought she was probably having second thoughts about inviting Jaclyn, but it was too late now. "I like the light-hearted trick-or-treat part of Halloween, not the Stephen King murder-y part."

Jaclyn shrugged. "You can't pretend it doesn't happen."

"Sure I can," Josie said, but her gaze clouded and I knew

she was thinking of the deaths that had happened in Bliss since I'd been back. Not that I'd brought them with me—although I had been wondering if my Cassidy charm was less about sewing the hopes and dreams and wishes into the garments I made for people and more about...death. I'd seen my fair share of it, and so had Josie.

Jaclyn didn't seem willing to let the subject drop. "It happens, Josie. There are bad people all around us. Hell, there are probably bad people in this very room," she said, her eyes skimming over us all, with an extra beat on Yolanda. I bristled on behalf of Josie's grandmother. She had been fiery in her youth, yes, but bad? No.

I snuck a glance at Juletta. I didn't think she was inherently bad, just as Orphie wasn't, but I had to admit that Jaclyn had a point. We all had the capacity to do bad things— some by design and some for self-protection.

Jaclyn's words slowed. "And I bet we've *all* seen something bad happen...even if we didn't realize it at the time."

"What are you talking about?" Rowena asked, her low and monotone.

"Yeah," Abby said, eyes bugging. "You're kinda creeping me out."

Jaclyn just shrugged. "All I'm saying is that I've seen some things that are...shall we say, questionable? I bet y'all have, too."

"What, like seeing somebody shoplift?" Juletta asked, a glint in her eyes. "Guilty."What she'd tried to do to Orphie was right up there with stealing from a store. Worse, maybe.

I scowled at Juletta and she clamped her lips shut and gave an innocent shrug.

"I get what she's saying," Madison said to the room. "Believe me, *I've* seen plenty of bad. High school students? Most of them are great, but there are a few..."

She bit her lower lip, stopping herself from finishing the

rest of that sentence. Bliss was a small town and everybody knew everything. I was sure she didn't want to say anything overtly disparaging about her students, especially with Holly, Libby, and Gracie in the room.

Jaclyn lifted one shoulder, her expression clearly saying, *whatever*. "Sure. Shoplifting. Wayward kids. You name it. Money laundering—"

"Like Ozark!" Holly said.

"Sure. Like Ozark. Or car theft. Identity theft. Fraud. And —" And then she paused, almost for dramatic effect. "—*Murder.*"

Abby and the three teenagers all gasped at the same time. "Murder?" Gracie murmured, wide-eyed.

Rowena jutted her chin forward, her bangs falling back into her eyes. "Wait, you said we've all seen bad things, even if we didn't realize it. Are you saying..." Her voice lowered to a hoarse whisper. "Are you saying you *saw* a murder? Like actually witnessed it?"

Jaclyn squeezed orange icing from the bag she held, nonchalantly, as if she wasn't saying something utterly jaw-dropping. She gave another of those one-shoulder lifts. "Maybe. Every time someone dies, I think, what if it was murder? Did someone have something to gain? Or did someone have something to cover up?" She paused to look up, her eyes scraping over each of us in turn, and then she spoke slowly, as if she were thinking aloud, pondering her own words. "You know what they say about hairdressers, prostitutes, and bartenders."

If Holly, Libby, and Gracie had been sitting down, they'd be on the edges of their chairs. "What do they say?" Holly asked breathlessly.

Jaclyn lowered her voice to match and answered conspiratorially. "We're all good listeners and people tell us their secrets."

"So you have a collection of stories people have told you," Rowena said. "And one's about murder?"

The corner of Jaclyn's mouth lifted in a smug smile. She didn't answer but the message was clear. She had, indeed, heard about a murder.

We all inhaled in a collective breath. Madison spoke first, her voice tight. "Someone actually told you about a murder?"

Again with that puffed-up expression. "Sure did."

Juletta leaned forward. She didn't know these people, but her curiosity was clearly piqued. "Who?"

Jaclyn's expression suddenly changed and she looked chagrinned. "Oh my gosh, y'all, I shouldn't have said anything. Halloween does this, right? Brings out the *spooky*. All I'm saying is that you never know. Sometimes things are not what they seem."

"Oh my god," Holly said, staring at Jaclyn with bug eyes. "What about that woman who died last week on the Pacific Coast Highway? Could that have been...do you think she could have been..."

"Now *that* was tragic," Jaclyn said. "And you pose a very good question, Holly. *What if?*"

The color had drained from Madison Blackstone's face and she looked more ghost-like than human. "Oh my...what if her brakes were bad and that's why she went over the edge?"

Abby Lassiter visibly shivered. "Drowning like that? In that cold water?" She shook her head so hard that her ponytail whipped around to both sides of her face. "I can't even imagine. It's so terrible."

"So, what if it wasn't an accident?" Jaclyn posed. "I think about those things, you know—"

"Why?!" Abby squealed. "That is *so* dark, Jaclyn."

She pursed her lips before saying, "Life is dark," then she exchanged her bag of orange icing for a purple-y black one and

23

started piping curved triangles and toothy grins onto the pumpkin shapes already covered with orange.

A few of the women, including Juletta, muttered their agreement. The tension in the room was thick like morning fog. It lessened, just a touch when Rowena let out a "*Mwaha-haha...*" followed by a blank-faced, "Life is dark. Death is in the air."

Abby blew out a shaky breath. "Too. Freaky." She glanced at Josie. "I should probably get your grandmother home."

No one said anything for a moment. Finally, Josie nodded, then broke the silence with a clap of her hands. "Come on, y'all. This is Halloween, like *Hocus Pocus*, not *Pet Sematary*. We have cookies to decorate and pumpkins to paint."

"They try to kill the children in *Hocus Pocus*," Rowena said dryly, to which there was a low murmur in response.

Abby headed to where Yolanda sat, but the old woman slowly shook her head. Her eyes were wide. It was clear she wasn't going anywhere, so Abby turned around.

"It's Josie's house. So let's talk about something else. Let's go around the room and tell what your costume is," Madison said, forcing a smile. She was still pale, but she flipped her blond hair away from her face and tried to smile. It was a valiant effort to change the subject. "I'll go first—"

"No!" Josie's voice rang out, cutting Madison off. Everyone's gaze swung to stare at her. "I want it to be a surprise," she said. "At the party. You know, so we can *ooo* and *ahhh* at each other. I mean, how often do we get to do this?"

Another wave of agreement went up and Josie gave a grateful nod.

"Babe," a man's voice said.

Abby's gaze darted to the wide open space of the firehouse's living room and the man walking toward them. Her demeanor changed in an instant to giddy and in love. She raced to him.

"Baby!" She slipped her arms around his waist and tilted her head back, smiling up at him. "You came! I almost left to take my patient back home. Oh my god, I'm so glad you're here."

The young man stood close to six feet, splayed one hand across Abby's back, and dropped a kiss on her forehead. "Got off early." He raised one hand in greeting. "Hey, I'm Miles." A chorus of greetings flew back at him. He chuckled and squeezed Abby's shoulder. "Now, what are you mockingbirds chittering about?"

Abby lowered her chin and peered up at him through her lashes. "Death," she said in a quivery whisper, fiddling with her necklace.

Miles drew his head back in surprise. His gaze scrabbled over each of us, then it hitched on the Halloween sugar cookies and he raised his brows. I wasn't sure if he was trying to merge the fun, festive mood in the kitchen with the morbidity of death or if he just wanted a cookie. "What kind of death?" he asked.

Abby swatted his arm, trying to play it off lightly. "The kind where someone dies, silly." She lowered her voice to a whisper and looked up at him through her lashes.

Rowena folded her arms like armor over her chest."Like, someone mentioned the woman who drove off the cliff. What if that was *murder* is the question."

"No, it's *not* the question," Josie exclaimed.

"But it might be," Madison said.

Miles drew his head back and gave a forlorn whistle. "I thought it was...er that she..."

"Ran off the cliff on her own," I said, filling in the part of that sentence that was so hard to just blurt out.

He winced. "Right. Sorry. Not easy to just *say* that."

Jaclyn looked up from the cookies. "So true. Murder is *so* much better than suicide," she said sarcastically.

Miles threw up his free hand, palm out. "Whoa. I'm not saying that. Neither one is good."

Abby pointed at Jaclyn. "*She* thinks it was...*murder.*"

Jaclyn pulled her lips tight. "Hey, I just...hear things," she corrected. "And I ask, what if? From what I know, that woman didn't have a reason to off herself."

"So much for small towns being safer than the city," Juletta murmured from beside me.

Madison Blackstone picked up her icing back. "Her name was Carrie Templeton. She was in PTA with my mom...back in the day. She was a nurse at Mercy. In the ER, I think. Her son teaches at the high school. And I think we need to show a little respect."

"I bet we all know someone who knew her," Rowena said, ignoring Madison. "What's that game...five degrees of separation?"

"Seven," Jaclyn said, tucking a strand of her straight brown hair behind one ear. She lifted her chin up, which raised her already upturned nose even higher.

Madison sighed and shook her head, frustrated. "No, no. It's six degrees to Kevin Bacon."

Rowena did jazz hands. "Separation. Kevin Bacon. Whatever. It doesn't matter. I'm just saying, she was local, so we all probably know *someone* who knew her."

I had to agree. The odds were pretty good. Bliss was a small town, and if the woman had been in PTA at any point, then people most certainly knew her. I felt my expression turn grim. "I doubt we'll ever know for sure what happened," I said.

Abby stepped out of her boyfriend's embrace and gestured widely to include everyone in the kitchen. She looked at Jaclyn first. "I don't know her, and I don't know anyone who was actually murdered," she said, then muttered under her breath, "And you're seriously twisted." Louder, she said, "What about the rest of you? I'm sure none of you has actually known anyone who was actually *killed,* right?"

A chorus of "no" sounded, but I abstained. The fact was, I had known *several* people—*more* than several, actually—who'd died suspiciously, and I'd had a hand in bringing the murderers to justice.

Beside me, Juletta stood up straighter and threw her shoulders back. She looked at Miles and arched her brows with curiosity. "Have *you* known anyone who was...murdered?"

I stared at her, aghast and frowned, not liking the saucy look she tossed his way. I'd hoped Juletta had changed, but maybe she hadn't. Flirting with a man in the presence of his girlfriend wasn't the same as stealing from a colleague, but both were pretty bad in my book and spoke to her character. On top of Abby standing right there, the guy was also way too young for her—Cher and her boy toys notwithstanding. Plus the question and this whole conversation just felt wrong. Flippant. Death, after all, was no laughing matter.

But Miles couldn't read my mind and apparently, he didn't feel the same way I did because he gave a little shrug as he said, "I have actually."

Juletta gaped up at him, nonplussed. It was clearly *not* the answer she'd expected. "Really?"

From the goggle-eyed expressions everyone in the room wore, they were just as surprised by that admission as she was. Myself included.

Abby waved her arm to calm everyone down. "He's an EMT," she said. "Of course, he's seen people die."

"Unfortunately," he said. "It does happen more often than you might think. You definitely can't save everyone. And I kind of agree with—" he pointed to Jaclyn for a second— "with you. All of you probably know someone who's been... you know, the victim of a murder. Macon Vance?"

Abby clasped the pendant swinging from her necklace as

she let out an edgy giggle as if the entire conversation was filling her with nervous energy, but then she suddenly dropped her hand and snapped her fingers. "That's right!" She pointed at me. "Weren't you there when he was killed?"

This was how rumors started, so I quashed it right away. "Well, not while he was actually *being* killed—"

"What about that guy who played Santa Claus. *That* was sad." Rowena eyed me. "Wait. You were there for that, too, weren't you?"

Everyone moved back a quarter of a step as if they were afraid a switch might flip and I might go postal on them.

I couldn't actually blame them because it was true. Sad and tragic. And I *had* been present when *that* poor man met his demise. "Every single murder is terrible—"

"Pft."

The sound had come from Jaclyn and I was grateful for the distraction. We all spun our gazes to her. "Some people deserve to die," she said, and then, when no one agreed, she prompted with, "Come on. People who *steal* or *cheat* or *lie*, and when those things affect other people? And what about greed and revenge and people who screw over someone else? They *should* be held accountable."

"That's what the justice system is for," Miles said.

Abby smiled up at him. "His dad's a lawyer," she said, her pride by association evident.

"I'm with Miles," Madison said. "It's not our place to play judge and jury."

"Exactly," Miles said.

I had to agree with them both. Despite Texas history, vigilante justice was not the way a society should function.

Jaclyn spit out another *Pft.* "Seriously? The legal system? Half the time it doesn't work."

"Jaclyn," Josie said, "please, stop."

Jaclyn whirled to face Josie. She was full of vinegar and

piss. "Stop what? People get away with bad behavior all the time. It's a fact. That's all I'm saying. They get away with stuff. All. The. Time. And they shouldn't."

The frown on Josie's face deepened. "No, they don't. I've *seen* the justice system work."

That was also true. Josie had been embroiled in her own sordid mystery not so long ago, but Lady Justice had prevailed in that instance. Still, Jaclyn's statements sounded personal. "Like who?" I asked, shooting a glance at Josie, silently telling her to calm down. "Who gets away with stuff?"

"Okay, look," Jaclyn said. "I *know* a guy who screwed over so many people. A small-time publisher and a total and complete crook. This lady I know—"

"A client?" Rowena asked.

Jaclyn flashed her a *so what* look. "As it happens, yes. Anyway, she wrote a children's book—"

"Oh my god, that's so cool," Holly said. "I want to be a writer!"

Jaclyn grimaced. "Yeah, well, from what my client told me, it's not all it's cracked up to be, let me tell you. She thought getting it published meant she had made it. Um, no. She said her book died a slow death because that sleaze and his company didn't do their job. They didn't promote it or market it or do anything to help it sell. She tried to get the rights back to it...*her* book...for two years. Two. Years. He kept saying no. Just no, without any explanation. And apparently, he did that to almost everyone stuck in a contract with him. Woman-hater, that's what I think."

"What did she do?" Josie asked, wide-eyed.

"She sued him. Small claims court, and this is what she told me. Even though the judge saw what the guy was doing... he actually told her after it was over that the guy was a crook— my friend's word, not his, but that was the message—but because she had signed the termination agreement, which *he* only finally signed when she *threatened* to sue, *that* superseded the original contract, so even though the guy owed her for whatever money he collected over the two years he held *her* intellectual property hostage, she'll never get a dime of it. It's a freaking paradox to the Nth degree. He's scum. Of. The. Earth. So forgive me if I don't put a lot of stock in the justice system. Not that she'd've been able to collect even if she'd won. I mean, apparently, he was bouncing checks left and right—"

"Whoa," Miles said. "Really?"

"Yep."

"I'm pretty sure that's a criminal offense in the state of Texas. You can't just bounce checks."

She scoffed. "Right, but who's going to stop him?"

"My dad worked on a case like that. If it's reported, the sheriff'll go out there and slap handcuffs on the guy and haul him to jail. Doesn't matter how much they're for or if it's ever made right, you can't write bad checks. It's a crime, period, the end."

Abby beamed up at her boyfriend. "I think Miles should go to UT Law someday," she said, but Jaclyn wasn't impressed. "At this point, it doesn't matter. She's done with him."

"But we have to fight the good fight," Madison said.

Jaclyn rolled her eyes so hard I thought they might get stuck at the top. "There's no *we* here. She lost, end of story. Sometimes the good fight doesn't matter. And that's what I mean. Some bad people are just pure bad and they get what they deserve."

"But the good fight has to matter," Josie said. "Madison's right. None of us can give up when we know what's right."

Jaclyn threw up her hands. "But that's just it, isn't it? My client? She knew she was right, but the judge had to find in the jerk's favor."

"She didn't lose because she wasn't right," Madison said.

"It sounds like it was because of contractual law. Is it unfortunate? Yes, but that doesn't negate the fact that your friend or client was still right. And *that* guy? He's been put on notice. He knows he can be sued now, and that it could happen again."

"It doesn't matter. That's over," Jaclyn said. She cleared her throat and her left eye twitched. She looked at each of us in turn. "Anyway, back to what I was saying earlier. Sometimes what you think you're seeing isn't what you're actually seeing. Only later does the truth hit you."

No one seemed to know what to say to this. Was she thinking about something specific, or speaking broadly? Either way, the woman seemed a little bit off her rocker.

After an uncomfortable silence, Josie clapped her hands to redirect the conversation to a happier, less haunting topic. "Come on, y'all. That's enough of that. We're getting ready for a party."

Madison and Rowena looked at each other. Juletta, Gracie, Libby, and Holly looked shell-shocked. Miles pulled Abby close, wrapped his arm around her, and whispered something in her ear that made her giggle.

Before any of us could say, "Boo!" Jaclyn threw up one hand in a halfhearted wave. "I'm outa here," she said. Her heels clicked against the hardwood floor as she made her way to the front door. After it closed with a thud, the entire room seemed to exhale the breath it had been holding. I wondered what Jaclyn's wishes and dreams were, and if I could design something for her to wear so maybe she could be a little less jaded, but nothing came to mind.

The damper on the party prep was solid and a short time later, one by one, the others left, too. Abby, who still looked spooked, led a very tired Yolanda back out to her car. Miles fell into step beside them. Next, Madison scooted off, and finally Rowena. Holly, Libby, and Gracie had gone off to play with

Molly, and I finished stringing cobwebs while Juletta munched on a cookie. "She better not ruin the party!" Josie wailed.

"She won't," I told her and gave her arm a bolstering squeeze. "It'll be fine. Better than fine. Great. It's going to be great!"

Josie didn't look convinced, but I reassured her with a hug. It wasn't until I was in bed for the night that my thoughts drifted back to the afternoon at Josie's. After the brouhaha, Juletta and I had come back to Buttons & Bows. I'd offered her one of my guest rooms and now she was tucked in like a bug in a rug...but I still didn't know why she was here.

I replayed the scene in Josie's kitchen. My brow furrowed as I realized that I hadn't pictured any of the women in designer outfits. I'd started to with Jaclyn, but nothing had come to me. And I hadn't envisioned anything for any of the others, except for a burst of color for Yolanda. Since I'd discovered it, my charm had been tried and true...until today. What did it mean? Had my well run dry? A chill swept over my skin and I pressed my interlaced hands to the top of my head. A jolt of frenetic energy coursed through me. The creeping feeling that maybe there was a dark side to my Cassidy charm deepened. If I couldn't picture the perfect garment for someone, did that mean they were going to die? Was that part of my charm? Being able to predict death?

A shudder passed through me as that thought took hold and the spot at my temple where a tuft of hair grew platinum, a stripe of blond against the dark, tingled. The doors to my closet swung open slightly, then banged shut. The window wasn't open, so no breeze circulated. A mournful sound drifted into my consciousness and filled the darkness. Loretta Mae. "Is that it, Meemaw?" I asked the ghost of my great-grandmother. "Is that part of my charm? Do I force someone's death?"

But I hadn't seen a garment for *any* of the women today.

Not one. Did that mean they were *all* going to perish? Was Josie's house going to burn down with all of us in it? Were we all doomed?

"Haaarrrlllloooowwwww." The soul-stirring sound took up all space in the room, the two syllables of my name stretching into something long and haunting. It was the best she could do at communicating. I had no idea if Loretta Mae had answered my question with her low lamentation. I asked her again, but the curtains fluttered for a moment before falling still. I put my glasses on the nightstand. "Goodnight, Meemaw," I said into the empty room. I shivered, even though it was toasty under the weight of one of my great-grandmother's quilts.

Chapter Four

My atelier used to be the farmhouse's dining room. White wainscoting ringed the space. Meemaw's old Singer sat on her equally old sewing table against one wall. My much more modern Pfaff was under the window overlooking the front yard and the pecan tree that canopied it. The roses should have been past blooming, their dead-looking branches reaching toward the gloomy sky, but Mama's magical green thumb kept them lush even in October. A mass of twining, heart-shaped leaves, and a riot of delicate bright pink flowers of Mexican Coral Vines scrambled over the fence and arched arbor separating the sidewalk from the yard. A patch of Bluebonnets, which were also past their blooming season, spread over the right side of the yard in a blanket of cobalt. Tessa Cassidy's charm kept my yard in an abundance of flowers no matter the season. Sage, snapdragons, pansies, asters, and cornflowers raged on either side of the flagstone path leading from the arbor to the front door.

As the sun rose, painting the sky in watercolor splotches, my foot depressed the pedal of the Pfaff. My gaze returned to the black organza I gently fed under the presser foot. The needle moved up and down like it was eating the fabric, bit by bit. I worked almost without thinking. My costume was practically creating itself—thank god, because my mind was elsewhere.

I removed a thin pin from the organza and tucked it between my lips next to the three others already there. Not a good practice and one Meemaw had always tried to break me of, but I was too distracted at the moment to care. Echoes of Jaclyn Padeski's stories reverberated in my mind right next to visions of Carrie Templeton's car plunging over the cliff and into the Pacific. The party preparations at Josie's had started out fine, but the conversation at the end had stayed with me all through the night and into the morning.

A few minutes later, Orphie Cates blew in like a gust of warm air. She was a designer, but honestly, she could have been a model. She was *that* beautiful. Dark skin. Black hair. Defined cheekbones. Legs that went on for miles. She stood a good few inches taller than me, and with her heels on—which was almost always, she was taller still. Total model material. She was electric, bringing instant energy to the room. "Good morning, sunshine!" she sang, her beautiful eyes glimmering with excitement. She carried two cups of steaming coffee from Villa Farina, the Italian café on the square.

Earl Gray squealed at my feet, trying to jet out the front door by darting between my legs. Orphie blocked him as she slipped in and handed me one of the cups. "You read my mind," I said, taking a sip of the pumpkin latte, cradling it between my chilled hands.

"It's my superpower," she said. Her gaze scanned the room, dancing over the Prêt-à-Porter rack, the velvet settee, and the accordion divider I used to create a dressing room in the corner. Garments hung from it on velvet hangers. Everywhere you looked, my designs shined. She walked past me to peer into my workroom, and through the archway that led to the kitchen. Then her eyes landed back on me and they opened wide, her chin dipping toward her chest. "Is she here?"

I stared. Surely she didn't mean Juletta. She didn't even know our old coworker was here. Loretta Mae, then? But it's not like we talked openly about my great-grandmother's otherworldly existence. "Who?" I asked.

She cocked her head to one side. "I know," Orphie said as if she'd literally read my mind.

"You know what?"

"Come on Harlow. I *knowwww*," she repeated.

I stared, open-mouthed. "How?" I asked, but I knew the answer. Bliss, after all, was an itty bitty Southern town where gossip traveled faster than a shooting star in the night sky.

"Josie told Nate who told Gavin who told me," she said.

Ah, so she *was* talking about Juletta. I shook my head and pointed to the staircase. "Still asleep."

Her eyes widened. "Right. She never was a morning person, was she? Did she tell you why she's here?"

"I asked her, but she won't tell me. It's like it's a big secret," I said, although I was beginning to wonder if Juletta knew that Orphie now lived in Bliss and if *she* was the reason for the visit. Was she going through a recovery program? Was Orphie on her list of people to make amends to?

We didn't have to wait long to find out the answer. Moments later Juletta glided down the stairs, eyes half-mast. She moved as if she were following the enticing aroma of coffee wafting in an invisible ribbon. She saw me and gave a little nod.

Then she spotted Orphie and froze.

And there was my answer. She *was* here because of Orphie.

Orphie spied her at the same time. She smiled and held one of the disposable cups out. The color drained from Juletta's face and for a second I thought one of her dizzy spells might be starting, but she took a breath and jerked into motion again, finishing her descent, reaching for the cup, and slipping into a hug with Orphie at the same time.

"It's good to see you," Orphie said.

"You, too." As they separated, I stood back and sipped my steaming drink, watching them as if they were actors in a two-person play.

Orphie's expression turned more somber. "Juletta," she started hesitantly. Juletta waited expectantly until Orphie continued. "Where did you go when you left Maximillian? *Why* did you leave...and without saying goodbye?"

Juletta blinked her eyes closed and pressed the side of her coffee cup to her cheek as if to warm a chill that had swept through her. I knew the truth, but would she confess to it?

Her lids suddenly flew open and she stared at Orphie. "C-can I...can I talk to you?" She glanced at me and then back to Orphie. "Privately?"

Orphie raised her brows as she shot me a baffled look, but she nodded. "I can go work in the atelier," I said. "Finishing touches on my costume."

I retreated, sat at my Pfaff, and tried to concentrate on the black organza and not the hushed voices coming from the Buttons & Bows showroom. My foot lifted off the pedal and the rapid-fire sound of the sewing machine needle moving up and down, up and down, up and down stopped.

I leaned back, sipping my coffee as their voices rose and fell. I caught some of the conversation—mostly Juletta apologizing, but then my jaw dropped when Orphie confessed to her own theft of Maximillian's LookBook. I didn't think she'd ever bring that up. Their voices faded as a quiet tap tap tap sounded from outside on the porch. That blasted woodpecker was back and striking its beak against the wood siding of the house. I wanted to bang the wall to get it to stop, but I couldn't pinpoint the location...and there was no way I was going to disturb the conversation Juletta and Orphie were having. Once they were done talking I could go outside and chase it away. But then it stopped suddenly and just like that, the echoing sound of it in my head stopped, too.

It was quiet. Were Juletta and Orphie still talking? I tilted my head one way, then the other, in case one ear could pick up sound better. I thought I heard crying, and I was able to make out a few random and disconnected words: *threatened, designs, had to leave, Maximillian, LookBook, Harlow.*

I started. Which one had said my name, and why?

I didn't have to wait long to find out. Their low voices stopped and a few seconds later the bells hanging from the knob of the front door jingled as the door opened, then clicked closed again. I glanced out the window and saw a woman hurrying down the sidewalk away from town. Something about her was vaguely familiar, but I forgot about her when my gaze caught Juletta striding down the porch steps and over the flagstone path. At the arbor gate, she turned left, heading toward town.

The clickity-clack of Orphie's heels against the hardwood floor grew louder as she came back into the atelier. I spun to face her, knowing full well how guilty I probably looked. She didn't seem to notice—or else she didn't care that I'd tried to ear hustle. Her eyes were red-rimmed and dark half-moons had appeared under them. The change from how she looked when she'd first arrived was alarming and I jumped up. "Orphie?"

Her lips quivered and she swiped at a tear trailing down her cheek. "You knew," she said, her voice shaky.

"I...what?" I stopped because of course, I knew exactly what she was talking about.

"She tried to steal my designs. That's why she left so suddenly. And you knew."

There was no way to deny it so I dipped my head in a contrite nod.

She shivered as a chill wound through her, and she

wrapped her arms around herself. I caught a shift in the air behind her. Saw the air ripple. I furrowed my brows, watching a figure start to form out of thin air. Meemaw. She was here and moving closer to Orphie with each passing second. Her spectral powers were getting stronger. More refined. I didn't know if she'd ever be like Moaning Myrtle in Harry Potter, looking more real than not, but she was certainly trying.

The translucent shape floated until I thought it had to be touching Orphie's back. Orphie blinked. Jerked. And for a split second, it seemed as if she went away. As if her body turned into a hollow shell with no life in it. Then she blinked again and her eyes locked on me. At that moment, I saw something different in Orphie and I *knew* Loretta Mae had made contact.

The glassy-eyed distress painted on Orphic's face seconds before was gone. In its place was a mischievous glimmer. Her mouth spread into a delighted smile. "Sweet pea," Orphie said.

I froze, my mind hurtling back to my teenage years when I'd spent hour after hour after hour in the farmhouse with Meemaw, and when she'd used her pet name for me. "What did you call me? Orphie?"

"Sweet pea," Orphie said again, her smile growing even bigger if that was possible. "And darlin', you best close your mouth or you'll catch some flies."

My skin turned hot, burning from the inside out, and my eyes felt like marbles ready to burst from their sockets. It was Ophie's voice...but those were my great-grandmother's words. My voice dropped to a hoarse whisper. "*Meemaw*, is that you?"

"It sure it, Suga—"

She broke off as Orphie's eyes flew into a frenzy of rapid blinking. It was as if she were a robot with a short circuit. "Whaaat the—"

The voice came out braided together in a haunting combination of Loretta Mae's and Orphie's. I didn't know who to talk to. "Meemaw!" I yelled. Orphie's lids spasmed again, her pupils rolling up...up...up. "Oh my god, Orphie?!"

I gripped her arms and gave her a little shake. "Meemaw, stop!"

"Darlin'—"

"Loretta Mae Cassidy!" I barked it this time, grabbing ahold of Orphie's shoulders. "Stop this!"

"I'll be ba..." Meemaw trailed off as a violent shudder coursed through Orphie. The frenzied eye movement increased and then came back to the center. With a sudden jerk, she lurched back and out of my grip. At the same moment, the air in front of her rippled, and that invisible figure that had collided with her re-formed. Orphie's legs turned to rubber, her knees giving out. I lunged, throwing my arms around her and catching her before she collapsed. My mind tried to process what had just happened. My ghostly great-grandmother had been inside of Orphie for less than thirty seconds, and now she was out again.

Panic clenched my gut as Orphie stumbled back, breaking free of my grasp. Her head whipped this way and that, her eyes wild like a feral cat. Finally, they landed on me. "What just happened?" she blurted, spinning around, searching for some explanation for what she'd just experienced.

My mind raced with possible ways I could explain the moment. I could totally gaslight her. *Did you feel that? It was an earthquake*. Or... *You started to faint! Are you okay?*

Or I could go with the truth. My great-grandmother just did a crazy otherworldly possession thing where her ghost sort of took over your body and she actually spoke to me through you!

But Orphie didn't know about Loretta Mae's spectral state. Only Madelyn Brighton, who happened to be a paranormal junkie, had guessed the truth. How could I expect Orphie to understand that, apparently, all the Cassidy women didn't actually completely die...they became ghosts. It seemed to work like a game of tag. What I'd gathered is that a ghost remained a ghost until the next Cassidy woman passed through the veil, tagging her out and taking the previous ghost's place. What happened to the displaced ghost was anybody's guess. Mama and Nana had no idea, and Meemaw had never talked about this fun part of the Cassidy charm. All I knew was that whenever one of us died, we'd take Meemaw's place and she would cease to exist in the astral plane I now knew was a real thing.

My great-grandmother's attempted communication echoed in my mind. Conflict bloomed inside me. Had she become part of Orphie, possessing her like a demon, while Orphie became nothing more than a host? It had never crossed my mind that Meemaw might take possession of another person. Now I'd seen it happen and that poor person—in this case Orphie—had lost herself for a minute. What I didn't know was whether or not the ghost—in this case Meemaw—had been booted out by Orphie's inner power or if Meemaw had left on her own.

Before I could think of how to answer Orphie's question, she gasped again. Her eyes opened wide, the whites showing all around. Her fingers clawed at her chest. "It feels like my insides are all tangled up."

I gaped at her, speechless. It made sense. Meemaw had become tangible. A physical presence in the room. Would her form have displaced Orphie's organs? If so, would they go back to normal?

Orphie's gaze narrowed. She watched me and I could see her mind working. "Harlow. What. Just. Happened?"

How could I possibly answer that? *It was my great-grandmother, Loretta Mae. She's a ghost and she took over your body*

41

for a minute. She'd think I was plum crazy. And I wouldn't blame her for that.

I spent the next fifteen minutes fluttering around Orphie, convincing her to lie down on the settee. I made her a cup of hot tea, laid out a plate of shortbread cookies, and soaked a cloth in cool water. I perched on the edge of the barn door coffee table, still shaken by the Meemaw encounter—and *I* hadn't been the one half-possessed by a ghost. Orphie was recovering, though, and if she thought I knew what had happened to her, she didn't say so. Instead, she looked at me through sleepy eyes, the cloth on her forehead. "Do you remember Meghan Foxglove?" she asked out of the blue.

"Of course," I said. When we'd known her, Meghan Foxglove had been unforgettable. She dyed her hair brick red and kept the tips jet black. Both arms were covered in tattoos, and between her nose, ears, and eyebrows, she had a total of seven visible piercings.

"She and Juletta were roommates, remember? After Juletta left so suddenly, I asked her what happened. She told me that someone caught her sneaking around the workroom and poking around my designs. And that Juletta either had to quit and leave, or she'd get turned in."

I felt my face flush with the memory of my conversation with Juletta. The threat hadn't been quite so direct, but Orphie had gleaned the gist of it.

Outside, the woodpecker had gotten its second wind and was back with a vengeance. It pounded its beak against the house sounding like rapid gunfire. I tried to ignore it as Orphie gave me an earnest look. I felt my cheeks flame. She touched her own face as she looked at my red cheeks. Her mouth gaped. "Oh my God. It *was* you, wasn't it? *You're* the one that caught her."

Orphie was one of my closest friends. I hadn't come forward and told her what I knew about that time in our lives and that I'd caught Juletta—then or when she'd come to Bliss —but I hadn't actually lied to her. I couldn't—wouldn't— start now. Even if she hadn't just read it loud and clear on my face, I couldn't deny it. I leaned toward her and reached for her hands, clasping them between mine. "I wanted to tell you, but after she left, I figured it didn't matter—"

She sat up, the cloth falling from her forehead. She pulled one hand free, plucking it from her lap. I half expected to see an angry face but when she looked at me, her eyes were glassy and her lips quivered. "It didn't," she said. "It *doesn't*. And I did the same thing to Maximillian, and you...you..."

It was true, and it had been a shock to find out that she'd taken one of the famed designer's LookBooks, but once she'd done it, she'd regretted it. We'd solved the problem and figured out how to return the book to Maximillian and we'd moved on. "Water under the bridge, Orphie," I said. "That's all over."

She lay back and let the cloth cover her eyes again. Her breathing steadied and I could see her body relax. I left her to rest while I went back to my atelier to finish my costume. All the while, I wondered: Now that Juletta had come clean to Orphie, would she leave Bliss, or was she going to stick around?

Chapter Five

Juletta opted to stay home instead of crashing Josie and Nate's party. I thought that was just as well. Will, Gracie, and I bounced along in Buttercup, sitting side by side on the bench seat, each of us excited about our costumes. Josie was right. As adults, we didn't get to play dress up very often, and it was fun. Other than through the anonymity of their online persona, most people couldn't disguise themselves. But on Halloween—or for a Halloween party—you got to experience being someone—or something—else, if only for an evening.

Gracie sat in the middle between Will and me. She turned to look at me, letting her fingers dance over the long ebony and purple strands of my wig. "You make a pretty good Wednesday Addams," she said.

"Thanks." I'd decided on the costume before I'd met Rowena, who could have dressed up as the Addams' family daughter without putting in one ounce of effort. But it had been too late to change tacks. My costume—a black ruffled dress with a mesh bodice, black collar, a thin black leather belt, and black boots peeking out from underneath--had taken me a handful of hours more than I'd thought it would. I'd had to sew bias tape to the edge of all the lace, then do a loose pleat before sewing it onto the sheath that was the core of the dress. I wore a black wig with heavy bangs and two braids pinned up around my head. Will was also part of the *Wednesday* world. He was dressed in skinny black jeans and wore a royal blue sweat jacket underneath a royal blue and black jacket, its vertical stripes vaguely resembling a prison uniform. The *Nevermore Academy* emblem adorned the left side of the jacket, and a white button-down and tie in the same blue as the rest of the outfit finished the look.

"I like it, too," Will said, waggling his brows and smiling at me over Gracie's head.

I grinned right back at him, flicking up my temporarily darkened eyebrows.

Wednesday didn't wear glasses, so I tucked mine into the waistband of my dress. I could slip them on if my eyes got tired. The party was in full swing by the time we arrived. I scanned the room looking for familiar people, but with their costumes, identities were well disguised. Hercule Poirot and a Victorian widow filled plates with appetizers. A zombie and someone dressed as a banana milled around the punch table filling cup after cup after cup.

Blacklight cast a spooky glow over everything and a Halloween playlist of songs filled the house. The living room furniture had been rearranged to create a wide-open dance floor, but so far, no one was boogying. Will and I mingled, and then finally, a few minutes later, I spotted someone I knew. Even with her back to me, I recognized Orphie in her 1920s flapper dress. She was deep in conversation with someone I couldn't see, a cup dangling from one hand, a plate of food in the other. The Victorian widow strolled by—Sandra Allen, I realized. I waved and she nodded at me. Then I spotted Josie across the room. I wiggled my fingers at her, the opalescent black on my fingernails glimmering in the low light. I'd made her dress, and *wow*, if it didn't look amazing on her.

Gracie peered at her, and then her eyes flew open wide. She'd been around my atelier but I'd kept all the costumes under wraps. "She's one of the Sanderson Sisters from *Hocus Pocus*, right?" Gracie grinned. "Winifred!"

"Right!" I'd studied the dress Bette Midler wore in the original movie, then created a pattern using fashion designs from the 1600s. The bodice of the dress was green and purple with laces crisscrossing the center panel. It was tight-fitting, elongating to a point just below the waist. Full chemise sleeves, slightly puffed at the shoulders, ended with lacy flounces. Josie wore a corset rather than the actual boned bodice of the era, lifting her bountiful new mama cleavage. The tiny cartridge pleats at the waist helped the skirt hang perfectly. I'd finished it with a green velvet cape. The final touch was the fake teeth protruding from Josie's mouth, her pursed lips painted red. Gracie clasped her hands together, staring in wonder. "It. Looks. Amazing! God, I hope I can do that someday."

"Make clothes like that?" Will asked. "You already do."

It was true. Gracie had a gift. She was good with a needle and thread. Her charm was like mine in that it was connected to fabric and clothing. But unlike mine, images flew in and out of her mind from the clothing she wore or touched. She experienced bits and pieces of the stories of the people who had worn the clothes, or who had made them. Whatever I made for her didn't have that effect, and she was immune to clothes she made for herself. It had taken her a while, but finally, she was learning to control the charm and the power of the images that flashed through her mind.

Gracie skipped away to find Holly and Libby. One thing I loved about my future step-daughter, and fellow Butch Cassidy descendant, was that she still had a sense of innocence about her. So many teenagers went for the shock value of a sexy costume, but not Gracie. With her blue checked gingham dress, white apron, little basket, stuffed dog toy that resembled Toto, and braided hair, she *was* Dorothy Gale.

As Gracie disappeared into the kitchen, Josie and Nate strode toward Will and me. They looked even better in person than they had when they'd tried their costumes on at Buttons & Bows. Josie glowed in her Sanderson Sister dress, and Nate looked perfect as Thackery Binx, tousled in his brown pants and rumpled cream gauzy white shirt, the laces at the top loose. He carried a stuffed black cat. He was the man—and the stuffed toy represented who he became—Binx, the cat.

"Gorgeous!" I exclaimed, beaming at them. Josie put her hands on my shoulders, I put my hands on hers, and we grinned at each other. She pulled away, gave me a wink, then reached her arms toward me and wiggled her fingers as she burst out in song. "I put a spell on you, and now you're mine," she trilled.

Nate stepped back, holding his stuffed cat like it was a crucifix. He glanced furtively at Will and me. "We must stop them from finding the book and brewing their potion. We must stop them from sucking the life out of the children of Salem before sunrise!"

"It's a glorious morning. Makes me sick!" Josie said, quoting Winifred Sanford. She did have an abundance of great lines in the movie, more than the other two sisters combined.

"Damn, damn, double damn!" I said, channeling Winnie.

Will looked at three zombies staggering by, then out the window at the night sky. As his gaze came back to Josie and Nate, he flicked up his brows and lowered his chin. "It's a full moon outside. The weirdos are out."

"Will!" Josie screeched. "You know your *Hocus Pocus*. I'm so impressed!"

"I raised a girl," Will said. He bent at the waist and spread his arms wide, moving from side to side and sniffing. "I smell children."

Instantly, Josie bantered back. "I've always wanted a child. And now I think I'll have one...on toast."

"The house looks perfect," I said to Josie after they came back to the real world. The blacklight and spooky decor had upped the game since I'd seen it the day before. Maddison Blackstone sidled up. She looked like a teenager in low-rise jeans and a midriff-bearing t-shirt, her hair pulled into two low ponytails and topped with an olive green cap. I studied her, brows pulled together. "I give. Who are you?"

"Veronica Mars," she dismissed with a frown. "Not much of a costume, I know, but I love the show." She looked me up and down, waving one hand in front of me, then at Will. "You two look perfect. I love Wednesday. And that dress is amazing. It's exactly like the dress she wears on the show. Where did you *get* it? I want one!"

"She made it," Josie answered for me.

Madison backhanded Josie's arm. "She did not." She turned to me. "You did *not*! How did you *make* it?" she asked as if the very idea was unfathomable.

I started to answer, but Josie beat me to it. "Knowing Harlow, she spent hours and hours researching, then found the exact fabric, then made a pattern and...voila!"

"You made it," Madison said again, still flabbergasted.

"I did," I said. Any dressmaker worth her salt would be able to make it, but I appreciated Madison's compliment.

"I want to be Wednesday. Oh my God. I want to be Wednesday so bad. Will you make me one?"

I kept my expression grim in true Wednesday style and gave a slight shake of my head. "I'm afraid not. Instead, I will ignore you, stomp on your heart, and always put my needs and interests first."

Madison blinked in surprise, but a split second later she

guffawed. "From the show, right? That's something Wednesday says."

This time I did smile. "I memorized some of her doozies."

"Did you practice the dance?" Madison asked.

I got whiplash from the quick change of subject and I tilted my head as I looked at her, puzzled. "The dance?"

Madison gaped at me. "I mean, you watch the show, right? How'd you come up with the costume idea if you don't watch the show?"

I tried to keep a straight face and keep up the ruse, but a laugh escaped my lips. I winked and started to dance just like Wednesday did in the dance episode, making my body move in jerky motions, playing an invisible piano, and doing the Thriller.

Madison laughed and clapped while Josie grinned. "Harlow Cassidy, you are brilliant!"

I stopped, grinning as I brushed imaginary dust from my sleeves. "If you say so."

"I do. I definitely do."

"Oh, me, too," Madison said.

A new song started—the classic Zombie by *The Cranberries*. As the haunting tone of Dolores O'Riordin's voice singing about the troubles in Northern Ireland seeped into the space, the three zombies who'd passed us a moment ago trudged out to the makeshift dance floor and started a jerking dance.

I caught a glimpse of Orphie across the room. I wanted to wave to her, to flag her over to where we were, but she had her gaze down and looked lost in thought. My attention was drawn away from her by the frenetic zombies holding red Solo cups. "Who's that?" I asked, pointing at them.

Josie followed the invisible line of my hand and nodded. "I'm not sure. Creepy, right?"

Definitely creepy. They danced in a circle, the liquid in

their cups dangerously close to sloshing over the sides. Nate and Josie had moved the rug from the living room, so spills, at least, would be easy to clean.

She clapped. "I love it when I have to figure out who's who." She paused, then grinned, slipping into character again. "It looks like they've gone amok."

Oh! I laughed, jumping up and down like Sarah Sanderson from *Hocus Pocus,* and sang, "Amok! Amok, amok, amok, amok."

"They look good," Will said, prompting us all to take a closer gander.

He was right. They had done their zombie makeup expertly. Faux flesh peeled from their faces and their eye sockets were huge, eyeballs protruding. How had they done that? Their clothing, too, looked like it had been ripped right from dead and decaying bodies. Either that or straight off the set of The Walking Dead. It was impressive. If Josie and Nate were holding a costume contest, the zombies were strong contenders. "Very good."

Josie notched her head up at Nate. "Come, we fly!" she said and she loped away to join the others on the dance floor, Nate in her wake.

More costumed people crowded in as the Monster Mash played, followed by Bette Midler's rendition of I Put a Spell on You, and I suddenly felt like one of the bewitched people in *Hocus Pocus*, caught by a spell and enthralled.

Another song played, this one another Halloween staple—Goo Goo Muck, by The Cramps.

"The Wednesday dance!" someone hollered.

In a flurry, people lined up and started mimicking the dance moves—some of which I'd just done—Wednesday Addams did on the TV show. Will and I followed along. I was up to speed on the moves, but Will was always a beat behind everyone else who knew the dance. By the time it was over, we had collapsed into a frenzy of laughter.

A minute later, Gracie reappeared with Holly and Libby, who were both dressed as anime characters, in tow. They waved as they strode past us, then brushed away the cobwebs that crisscrossed in front of the French doors and went out to the side porch where a few people were tossing handheld beanbags at an old wood corn hole board.

I turned back to Josie. "You throw a spookalicious party—"

The words caught in my throat as a scream pealed through the air.

I spun around, trying to pinpoint where the scream had come from, but the beat of the music pounded, making it impossible. My gaze raked over the costumed people, searching for Josie, for Gracie, for Libby. For Holly. Josie shoved her way between a Thing One and Thing Two and appeared before me. "What was that?"

I felt the color drain from my face. Felt my hands go cold. Because it wasn't just any scream. It was the earsplitting, heart-pounding, something seriously wrong kind of scream.

I plucked my glasses from my waistband and threw them on, searching the crowd again. Where were the girls? Where was Gracie? And then I remember. "The porch!" I started to push my way through the crowd. Will was already moving, plowing through the people. I stayed in his wake. He yanked open the doors and flew outside.

"Daddy!" Gracie's shaky voice called to him, urging him toward her. "Hurry! It's..." She swallowed whatever words were on her tongue, instead just pointing to the ground at her feet where the bobbing for apples barrel lay on its side, the water that had filled it spilled over the deck, small puddles collecting on the four-inch boards making up the porch. The fruit that had been floating in the water was scattered around.

And there, on the floor and face down in the water, lay a zombie, a red apple lying by the side of his...or her...head.

Josie pressed her hands to her cheeks, panicked. "*Omigod, omigod, omigod!*" Every ounce of color had drained from her beautiful olive skin. It was pallid and almost as green as Elfeba Thropp, the Wicked Witch of the West. "Is...he...she...the zombie...*dead*?"

That was an oxymoron, wasn't it? Weren't zombies technically dead already? I pushed that thought aside as I dropped to my knees and pressed two fingers to the zombie's neck. I moved them around, searching. I detected a faint pulse, but then it was gone. My imagination, maybe, hoping for good news? But no, it was there. I flipped the body over and started chest compressions.

I stole a glance at the face, registering who was beneath all the creepy zombie makeup at the same moment those around me did. Josie shrieked. "Jac—! Oh my God, it's Jaclyn!"

"Is she alive?" someone hollered.

Will knelt down next to me. "Is she?"

"I thought I felt a pulse. So faint, but I think it was there."

A crowd had gathered and someone called out, "I called 911! They're on their way!"

I kept going, my hands interlocked, pressing down on her chest to keep the oxygen flowing, assuming I really had felt something.

The crowd surged forward, everyone itching to get a better look. Will jumped up and spread his arms wide, creating space. "Stand back," he said.

"Who is it?" someone asked.

"Yeah, did you see who it is?" another shaky voice echoed.

Clearly they hadn't heard Josie's wail.

Will didn't know Jaclyn, and Josie was sobbing. Nate stepped forward. "It's Jaclyn Padeski," he said. "Harlow's doing CPR until the first responders get here. Everybody, stay back."

With my peripheral vision, I saw Cleopatra, aka Rowena, elbow her way through the wall of costumed people until she stood next to me. With her black hair and heavy eyeliner, she played the Egyptian Queen perfectly. "I can take over for you," she said.

"I'm fine," I answered, never breaking my rhythm. I didn't want to let up even for a split second.

Bliss was a small town. It didn't take long for a shrill siren to pierce the night air. It grew louder and louder until the flashing lights of a patrol car and the deep roar of a firetruck's engine infiltrated the somber quiet of Josie and Nate's porch.

We all stepped back, making way for the volunteer fire-fighters and the paramedics. A woman dressed in a gray collared shirt, black boots, and dark cargo pants with multiple side-leg pockets dropped to her knees across from me. In my peripheral vision, I could see scissor handles sticking out of one of the pockets, along with the floppy fingers of a pair of latex gloves.

The other EMT knelt next to me, our legs touching, the edge of whatever tools were in his special pants pocket pressing hard against my outer thigh. He didn't spare me a glance, and I was too busy alternating between chest compressions and resuscitation, not even sure I was doing it right. It took only a long second for him to thread his fingers together, letting them hover over mine. "On three," he said, and then he proceeded to count, "One, two..." On three, I quickly backed away and he took over, picking up right where I'd left off. He was all business, not even looking at the party-goers. It's exactly how I wanted a paramedic to be If I ever needed rescuing.

The other EMT—a short, spry-looking woman with a patch on her navy jacket that read Ospry—stood and moved away from the body. She blew a sharp whistle through her lips. Everyone's attention shifted to her. "Let's everyone step back," she said, her arms spread wide to usher us away from the body. Everyone took a few steps toward the house, creating a semi-circle around the body and the EMT working on saving Jaclyn. A few party-goers went back into the house, still pulsing with music. Ospry came up to me. "Tell me what happened."

"The girls came outside," I said, gesturing vaguely toward Gracie, Libby, and Holly, who stood shivering at the corner of the porch. "We heard a scream and came running. As soon as we found her, I felt for a pulse and then started CPR."

The woman—Ospry—turned to her partner. "Did you find a pulse?"

"Faint," he answered. With his back still to us, he continued his rhythm of two rescue breaths, followed by chest compressions. Rescue breaths. Chest compressions. Back and forth, he repeated it, then pressed two fingers to find her carotid artery, just as I had. Went back to the compressions and breaths, then checked again. Any second now Jaclyn would sputter and drag in a deep breath. She'd open her eyes and try to sit up.

We all watched and waited with bated breath. But finally, the EMT sat back on his heels and shook his head grimly. The message was clear. Jaclyn Padeski was dead.

Chapter Six

I recognized the paramedic who had done his best to save Jaclyn Padeski when he turned to note the time of death to his partner. It was Miles, Abby's boyfriend, He had a long face and wore a heavy frown, shaking his head sadly. Ospry wore the same forlorn expression. Losing a patient they'd been discharged to save had to hit hard.

Watching their dispirited manner made my heart sink. Jaclyn Padeski was dead. I hardly knew her and I couldn't even say that I liked her—she'd come off so abrasively at Josie's house the day before—but now her life force was gone, drained away. I stared at the overturned barrel, apples scattered around her body. Her face and hair had been wet as I'd done CPR. Had she been bobbing for apples and lost consciousness? Was she so drunk that she drowned? Or had she experienced a cardiac incident, grabbing the barrel to steady herself, making it topple over instead?

Before I could come up with any more scenarios, Deputy Sheriff Gavin McClaine strode onto the porch. He cocked one eyebrow at the EMTs who nodded at him in a silent communication that conveyed the patient hadn't survived. His mouth pulled down in a heavy frown as he weaved through the costumed party-goers, finally making his way to the apple-bobbing barrel and the dead body. His ever-present smug expression still grated on me, although I didn't take it as personally as I used to. Gavin was a few years younger than me and I didn't think we'd ever spoken when we'd been in school. He'd been shyer than shy back then, and I'd always had one foot firmly out of Bliss and in Manhattan's fashion district.

How my now step-brother had won Orphie's heart was still a mystery to me, but he had. Granted, the guy was attractive in a self-satisfied, arrogant way. He'd gotten over his shyness and could win the prize for one of the most eligible bachelors in Bliss—now that Will Flores was off the market.

His white straw cowboy hat, piercing eyes, and cocky grin made him perfect for law enforcement. He wore his authority like a leather glove. Once again, Gavin gave a single look to the EMTs, followed by an upward notch of his chin. After a pronounced swallow—it seemed young Ospry wasn't immune to Gavin's countenance, even in the presence of a dead body— she cleared her throat and spoke first, relaying the 911 phone call and their arrival on the scene. Miles picked up the thread of the story, telling Gavin about Jaclyn's thready pulse. He gave credit to me for keeping up CPR until they arrived, his efforts once he took over, and Jaclyn's ultimate unresponsiveness. "There was nothing more we could do," he said.

Gavin asked a few follow-up questions, jotting things down in his notepad. There was no indication of foul play, but Jaclyn was young. I imagined he was wondering why she had died, just as I was. Finally, he crouched down at the body. With obvious respect, he looked at her—and then he flinched. I reckoned he hadn't expected the zombie face, distorted now from the water and CPR. He quickly schooled his expression and dipped his head in a respectful bow. Ospry had opened a yellow X-framed gurney. Gavin stood and backed away so

Ospry and Miles, could lift Jaclyn onto a gurney. They covered her with a sheet. Gavin sent them on their way with a wave of his hand. Miles shot a quick glance around the porch, pausing when he spotted Abby standing directly opposite of me. She had a cup in each hand and held one up as if she wanted to give it to Miles so he could bolster himself before leaving. Miles hesitated, looking for all the world like he wanted that drink, but finally, he shook his head. Right, because of course he couldn't just stop and take a drink.

With her deep frown, Abby's expression was resigned. She poured out the drink and nested her own cup in the now empty one. Miles had kept his gaze on her. He tried to smile at her through the grim look he wore, but he didn't succeed.

Madison Blackstone in her Veronica Mars jeans and cropped t-shirt sidled up next to me. "Was it a heart attack?" she asked, more rhetorically than actually seeking an answer, because, of course, no one knew.

"She looked healthy enough," I said.

She grimaced with a watchful eye on the EMTs as they wheeled away the gurney with Jaclyn Padeski's body on it. "Yeah, but you know what they say. Heart disease is the silent killer." Instinctively, I put my hand to my chest, feeling for my own skittering heartbeat. "I shouldn't speak ill of the dead," she said, half under her breath, "but I didn't really care for her."

I stared at her and she looked horrified, slapping her hand to her cheek. "I'm so sorry. I can't believe I just said that."

Honestly, I couldn't, either.

"I just...I..." She waved her hands, backing away. "Never mind. Forget I said that."

"It's okay. It's a shock," I said.

Once the EMTs were gone, Gavin scanned the porch. I could almost see his brain working behind his piercing eyes, registering everyone who was present, making a mental list of everything he'd observed so far. "Let me get this straight," he said. "The woman collapsed and you—" He turned and narrowed one eye at me— "performed CPR. At that point she was alive. The paramedics arrived and took over. A few minutes later, she was declared dead. Does that sum it up?"

Orphie slipped through the crowd. She wasn't smiling— all the effervescent bubbles of her personality washed away by the dead body—but I caught a quick glance and acknowledgment between her and Gavin, just as Miles and Abby had done a moment before. Love was still love, even under duress.

"That sums it up, Gavin," I said.

He kept his narrowed eyes trained on me, but this time I was pretty sure it was because I'd called him by his name instead of his title. Orphie must have sensed the tension because she moved toward him, reaching one hand out like she wanted to dance her fingertips over his arm. The man only ever wore his beige uniform and no matter how many times I'd tried, I'd never been able to picture him in anything else. Given that my Cassidy charm was doing just that—envisioning the perfect garment for a person, creating it, and thereby making their wishes and dreams come true, I was a little bit flummoxed by my inability to see Gavin in anything other than his deputy uniform. I didn't know what that meant. I didn't make many garments for men, but I'd seen Hoss in fancy clothes, and then sure enough, he'd married Mama in the very outfit I'd envisioned. I sometimes caught a glimpse of Will in something other than the jeans or Dockers he usually wore, but he had style and didn't need an upgrade. I absently spun the engagement ring encircling my finger. Meemaw finagling an introduction between us, not my charm, had made both of our wishes and dreams come true.

The music suddenly stopped and the background noise vanished. Without it, the sound of concerned talk in hushed voices grew louder. Gavin barked orders to the deputy and then spoke to the party-goers. "I suggest all y'all got on home. Not much to celebrate when someone dies in your midst."

Through the open French doors, I saw Rowena, Queen of the Nile, nod. She set her plastic cup down on a random table, pausing to gather herself together. She looked paler than normal and a little shell-shocked. Orphie's flapper dress threads swished past the deputy and came up next to me and Will. "It's really Jaclyn," she said as if she couldn't believe it. None of us had known the woman well. All our eyes were dry. But still, death was death, and a somber blanket lay over us.

When I looked back inside, Rowena was gone.

I raised my hand as if I were in a school classroom and I had a pressing question. Gavin glanced my way but didn't call on me. From somewhere inside, I heard Josie's shaky voice as she saw her guests out. "Take a bag. Bye. Yep, yep. So shocking. I'll see you tomorrow." In the distance, car doors slammed and car ignitions fired.

Finally, Gavin strode to where Orphie, Will, and I stood. He gave a quick wink to Orphie and I had to admit, the gesture was sweet. Even in the midst of death, he let her know he was also thinking about her.

"Why'd she die?" Orphie asked, still looking shell-shocked, a sallowness under her brown skin.

He shrugged. "Unknown."

"What was she, mid-thirties? She's so young," Orphie said, then quickly corrected. "*Was.* She *was* so young."

"She may have had a bad heart. A stroke. An illness. No way for us to know that."

There were plenty of people who died much too young because of unknown illnesses or diseases. I wondered if Jaclyn knew about the health issue that had ultimately taken her life.

Only an autopsy would tell.

Chapter Seven

The needle of my sewing machine moved up and down in a steady rhythm as I fed the black twill of the Hogwarts robe I was working on under the presser foot. I lightened the pressure of my foot on the pedal, slowing the speed and finally stopping at the corner. I'd set the needle to the down position, allowing me to turn the fabric and keep a clean corner. I depressed my foot and the machine charged into action again. I fed the fabric as the needle worked, stitching the lining to the robe itself.

The sound of pots and pans banging against each other came from the kitchen. "Meemaw!" I hollered. The clatter abruptly stopped and I could envision her ghostly form cocking one ear my way as she listened. "What in tarnation are you doing?!"

Of course, I knew she couldn't answer me. Juletta was out exploring the town square, so other than me, there was nobody here for her to inhabit—and even if there was, I didn't want a repeat of *that*. Seeing Orphie lose herself, even momentarily, was something I never wanted to see happen again—

even if it was the most promising way to communicate with Meemaw. There had to be a better option.

Meemaw responded with a low, haunting sigh full of frustration and unspoken words.

"I know," I said, leaving my sewing project to stand in the arched threshold between the atelier and the kitchen. The pots and pans she'd been clanging were scattered across the floor as if she'd thrown them in her vexation. The air rippled and I could make out where she hovered in her spectral state, but her shape didn't take form, and then the front door of Buttons & Bows flung open and the bell hanging from a ribbon jangled with more force than seemed possible. "Harlow!" Josie's voice bellowed, and with a silent pop, Meemaw's translucent shape vanished.

I spun around to Josie slamming the door shut behind her with one foot, Molly clinging to her side, her pudgy legs wrapped around Josie's middle, a diaper bag slung over her opposite shoulder. I hurried toward them, anxiety pooling in my gut. "What's wrong?"

She stopped short as the book she'd had tucked under her arm slipped, hitting the hardwood floor with a thud.

Josie stooped to set her daughter on the floor. She handed Molly a set of giant toy keys, each in a primary color. Molly immediately plunged one into her gummy mouth, sucking on it. "She's already teething, can you believe it?" Josie said, reaching for the book.

Earl Gray scurried past, catching Molly's eye. She let go of the toy keys and pointed to the teacup pig making a happy googling sound. "That's Earl," I said, crouching to retrieve the keys so I could rinse them before she stuck them back into her mouth.

Josie scooped up Molly, following me into the kitchen. I ran a burst of water over the keys, giving them a quick wash, then handed them back to Molly. She giggled and looked me straight in the eyes—and then she dropped them again.

"Molly!" Josie scolded, but only half-heartedly. She rolled her eyes. "It's her new game. She thinks it's hilarious."

It *was* pretty funny. I picked them up, cleaned them again, and started to hand them back, but Josie thrust Molly into my arms instead. She set the diaper bag on the table and retrieved a thin blanket, laying it flat on the floor. "There. Now you can put her down," Josie said.

I did, setting Molly in the center of the blanket and handing her the keys. She gripped them in her hands and then plunged them into her mouth again. Directly behind her, the air undulated, shifting from translucent to a weird half-opaque state. My stomach lurched as the blobby form moved closer to the baby. The hair follicles at my temple where my stripe of blond hair grew prickled as I launched myself forward, moving between Molly and my great-grandmother. "Stop!"

Josie gasped and lurched back. "Stop what?"

Meemaw emitted a moan and the thick air brushed against me. Jolted me. Seemed to move into me. I felt my body change —almost as if the air was viscous and that gooey element was filling the microscopic spaces between my cells.

Somewhere in the back of my mind, I heard Josie's voice and Molly's infant gibberish. "Harlow! What's happening? Are you okay?"

"Hello!"

Another voice. It sounded muffled as if it came to me through an ocean of salt water. "Harlow?"

"Oh my God, Orphie! Hurry! We're in here!"

Josie's voice. Then Orphie's, sounding so far away and more like a whale's song that I couldn't understand.

Meemaw! No! I felt myself say the words, but in my mind, not with my voice. Her voice, which I hadn't heard in forever, came back to me, an echo in my head. *I love youuuu, sweet pea...*

It was her. It was Loretta Mae. I sensed her presence in my body growing like a balloon filling up with air. Sound vanished. It was like being in a deprivation tank. The only sounds were the thump of my own heartbeat and the whoosh of my blood pulsing. My awareness of everything else evaporated. Tears pricked my eyelids. I *felt* her. She was with me now more completely than she'd been since I saw her last. She'd passed while I was laboring as part of Maximillian's designers, a low-level job that had nearly sucked the creativity out of me. And because of that job and my dream of being a fashion designer, I'd missed my great-grandmother's final months. Her presence as a ghost living in the farmhouse she'd given me the moment I was born, wasn't the same as talking to her. Touching her. Hearing her laugh. But feeling her entire being becoming one with mine was inexplicable. My insides expanded.

"Harlow?"

The sensation of sharing my body with another soul...with Meemaw...took my breath. *What's happening, Meemaw?*

I'm here with you, darlin', she said, speaking from far away, like she was in a dream. *I'm going now...*

Panic rose inside me. I didn't want her to leave. *No!*

Not forever, darlin'.

My blood turned cold. Like a balloon deflating, my body lost volume. A sob spilled out. *Don't go!*

You're a good girl, Harlow Jane Cassidy.

I miss you. I miss you. I miss you. The words filled me, taking the space she'd been in moments before and a wave of dizziness washed over me.

"Harlow!"

I was right about Will, wasn't I?

A surge of laughter rushed through me. Whatever Loretta

Mae wanted, Loretta Mae got. That was her charm, courtesy of Butch Cassidy and his wish in that Argentinian fountain. I wiggled my ring finger. *You were right.*

The pressure that had built with her presence inside me lessened.

The weight of two hands came down on my shoulders. As they shook me, I blinked. "Meemaw! Don't go!"

"Harlow!"

And then I was suddenly empty, my knees buckling, my legs giving way. Someone caught me under my arms. Kept me upright. Pushed me into a chair. I bent over, my glasses slipping down the bridge of my nose. I grasped them, yanking them off, and pressed my forehead against my legs.

"Harlow." It sounded like Orphie, but she wasn't here, was she? Josie was, with little Molly.

"Hey. Harlow." A hand rubbed my back.

I lifted my head to see Josie crouching in front of me. "Are you okay?"

Someone still rubbed my back. I turned my head. It *was* Orphie. I hadn't imagined hearing her voice. She *was* here!

"Loretta Mae," I murmured, looking around, searching the kitchen for a disturbance in the air. For any sign that she was still here. But everything was still.

"Harlow, seriously. Are you okay? Do you need a doctor?" Josie asked.

"Whaaa- what h-happened?" I asked, my mouth full of marbles.

Josie glanced at Orphie, then back to me. "It was crazy," she said. "It's like you went into a...a trance."

"Loretta Mae—" I whispered.

"What about her?" Josie asked.

I scanned the room again through foggy eyes. "Is she...here?"

Orphie's brows pulled tight. She laid the back of her hand

against my forehead. "You're not feverish, but you feel cold," she said.

Goosebumps popped on my skin. The sensation of Meemaw being part of me—of hearing her speak to me—it was already fading. Tears spilled from my eyes, sliding down my cheeks. Had it been real?

The front door opened, the bell attached to the grosgrain ribbon jingling. "I'm here, Harlow."

Will. Did we have a date?

"We're in here!" Josie hollered.

Seconds later, Will was there. He took one look at me then scooped me into his arms and told me that everything was going to be okay.

Twenty minutes later, I sat on the velvet settee in the Buttons & Bows showroom. Will, Josie, and Orphie gathered around me like clucking hens. Even Earl Gray perched at my feet. "I'm fine," I said for the fifth time.

"That wasn't normal," Orphie said. "You were in a trance and it was like you were talking to someone but nothing you said made any sense."

Josie frowned. "Except Meemaw. You said Meemaw a few times."

My cheeks heated but I didn't know if what I'd experienced was real or if I'd imagined it. "I just miss her," I said, shoving my glasses up to punctuate the statement.

Josie perched on the coffee table and bounced Molly on her legs. "Are you sure you're okay?"

I sighed, exasperated. Not with them, but with myself for not remembering what had happened. Then again, I'd witnessed Orphie go through something similar, if not quite so intense, and she remembered less. "Perfectly fine," I said. I turned my full attention to Josie. "Now, you said you wanted to show me something."

Josie eyed me skeptically, but she reached behind her with

her free hand and retrieved the book she'd had earlier. "I found this. It's Jaclyn's. It's a journal and--" She leaned forward as if she were imparting a great secret— "a ledger."

We all stared at her. Will frowned. "What do you mean, a ledger?"

Josie handed it to him. I stood at his side as he flipped through it, noting the pages and pages of straight up and down neat writing. Enviably lovely writing, but from the few words I gleaned, the content was less than lovely. Words like blackmail, silence, and paying for their crimes jumped out at me because they were bolded.

"Look in the back," Josie said.

Will flipped through toward the end of the book. "It's lists of names," he said, turning it around so we could all see the columns with dates, names, information, and dollar amounts.

"Look at these entries," Will said, tracing his finger down one of the columns. There was one for names, each printed neatly, all of them written in the same blue ink. Another column held cryptic notes that didn't make a whole lot of sense, one for a dollar amount, and another labeled PAID with a cursive pd.

"Was she blackmailing people?" I asked, frowning.

"Turn to the last page," Josie said.

Will did. The list continued, but the final four names were written in pencil. A blank line separated the list from the very last name.

It was that name that snagged my attention—and Will's. He looked at Orphie. "*Your* name is here."

Orphie stared at Will, then peered at her name written in neat block letters on the last page. The very *last* name written, in fact. "Theft," Orphie said, reading what was written in the third column. The final column, which for the other entries contained dollar amounts, was blank. "What the hell?" she muttered, her dark complexion suddenly drained of color.

I looked at the date listed next to her name, counting back. And then I gasped. That was the day Orphie and Juletta had been here, and they'd buried the hatchet about their past. It was the day of Josie's party.

But how...?

I thought about that morning, replaying it in my mind. I'd gone into my atelier to give them privacy. Something knocked against my brain. What was it? I tapped my head with my index finger, thinking. I'd been shocked when Orphie had confessed to Juletta, and then that tap, tap, tap had interrupted my eavesdropping. That dastardly woodpecker had tapped against the wall, the sound covering the details of the conversation happening in the Buttons & Bows showroom. It stopped, then came a few minutes later and attacked the wall with gusto, going at it like a machine gun. Then Juletta had left and Meemaw had tried to slip into Orphie's body.

"There's more," Josie said, pulling me back from my thoughts. She bent and pulled a small stationery envelope from the front pocket of her diaper bag. "This was tucked inside the pages."

"Should we be touching it?"

Josie shrugged uncertainly. "Probably not? But I already did."

I snatched a tissue from the box on the counter and took the envelope, using another tissue to open the flap and slip out the card fitted snugly inside, a note in the same neat cursive as the journal.

To Whom It May Concern,

If you have found this, it's safe to say something has happened to me. Of course I don't know what, or when, or by whose hand, but the pages of this book will direct you.

67

You may not agree with what I've done herein, but that's neither here nor there. If I was murdered, I want someone to bring that person to justice in the way I have done for others.

~Jaclyn Padeski

My head pounded as if that woodpecker had taken up residence in my skull, pecking away and scattering my thoughts. According to Jaclyn's own hand, she didn't just die. She was murdered.

Chapter Eight

The shock of Jaclyn's ledger, her note from the envelope, and Orphie's name listed there propelled me off the settee. I paced around my little showroom. I let my fingertips dance over the clothes hanging from the prêt-à-porter rack as I walked past. What was I missing? And then it hit me. I'd seen a woman hurrying down the sidewalk as Juletta left the house that morning. Brown hair. Average build. I hadn't given it another thought, but now...could it have been Jaclyn? Could she have come up the steps, planning to knock on the door and talk to me about something, only to stop and listen when she heard the conversation happening between Orphie and Juletta? All I'd heard was that woodpecker tap, tap, tapping against the side of my house. I hadn't heard anyone climb the steps, but that woman hurrying away...she had done just that. That had to be what happened. Jaclyn had come to Buttons & Bows for some reason. She'd listened as Orphie confessed about stealing Maximillian's LookBook. And she'd scurried away before anyone saw her. Later that day she pencilled Oprhie's name into her book probably figuring that would be a big payday for her. How much would Orphie have paid to keep her secret on the down low? "She heard them," I said.

Will, Orphie, and Josie stared at me. "Who's she, and what did she hear?" Orphie asked.

I spun to face them. "Jaclyn. She must have heard you and Juletta talking." I explained, telling them how I suspected Jaclyn had been on the porch and had overheard their conversation. They'd been too wrapped up in Juletta's confession to notice, and I'd been too wrapped up in trying to hear them over the woodpecker.

Orphie's jaw dropped. "You think she was planning on *blackmailing* me? So t*hat's* why...that's why my name is in her book? Does it say anything else?"

"Not about that," Josie said, her frown deepening, "but there's more. I skimmed through a lot of it. Look at the page I marked."

Will handed me the book and I flipped through until I found a pink arrow at the top corner of a page about three-quarters of the way through and toward the end of the journaling. I scanned the page and saw a second arrow, this one green. I skimmed the paragraph, sucking in a deep, troubled breath, then I reread it.

"What's it say?" Orphie asked. Her hands trembled in her lap and her lower lip quivered. She was taking her name being in Jaclyn's book hard.

I glanced at Josie, and she nodded. We both understood the potential impact of this. I read it aloud:

"One of my recent clients, for lack of a better word...after all, victim doesn't sound right, does it? As I was saying, one of my recent clients threatened me today. I mean, don't get me wrong. None of my clients are very happy when I reach out to them, but usually, our deals are cut and dry. I have my code, and I stand by my word. I love that part in *Pirates of the Caribbean* when Jack Sparrow is true to his character. Once a pirate, always a pirate. That's it in a nutshell. You can trust people to always be who they are. A zebra doesn't change its stripes.

"I'm a zebra, and I'm still striped black and white. I present my case, including the bill, and once payment is made, that's that. It doesn't matter how big or small the transgression is. Once it's paid, it's paid. I mark it off and I don't revisit it. I never go back and demand more.

"But my last client does not believe that. At all. It's all good, though. I'll make sure they understand the finite nature of our arrangement. They'll pay and it'll be over. I have other fish to fry, as the saying goes."

Orphie's breathing became labored. "Recent clients? I'm at the end of the list—"

"But she never contacted you," I said when she broke off.

Will tapped the journal in my hands. "We need to get this to the police."

The color drained from Orphie's face. "But...but...you don't think...they won't..."

"She *can't* be talking about you. Plus no one would believe you could possibly kill a person," I said. I thought about the other people who, from the lists and columns on the ledger, looked like they had already been extorted by Jaclyn. Only Orphie had no details and no payment information.

The book blew up the list of people with motives. The question was: *Who from that list had also been at the party?*

Will was right, the police *did* need this information. But before we called, I grabbed my cellphone, laid the journal open on the table, and snapped a bunch of pictures—all of the ledger with the names and money paid, and the page Josie had marked. "Did you read the rest? Was there anything else?" I asked her.

I expected her to say no, but instead, she nodded...her expression far too grave.

"What is it?" Will asked.

Orphie just stared.

Josie took the book and flipped to another random page she'd marked, this one toward the end but before the actual ledger portion. Holding it open, she turned it around. I took it. Read Jaclyn's notes. Gasped. Stared at Josie. "Seriously? All of them?"

Her nostrils flared as she gave a helpless shrug.

I looked at the page again.

Add:

ROWENA ADAMS?

ABBY LASSITER—$3000 ~~ASSOCIATION~~

MADISON BLACKSTONE—$6500 DUI

JOSIE KINCAID?

NATE KINCAID

Below that was another list:

DUI

DRUGS

THEFT

FRAUD

Will and I stared at the page, then at each other, finally turning to Orphie. "It's not just you," I said, holding the notebook out for her to see.

She rubbed her eyes and squinted at the page. "Oh," she said, then, "OH," finally ending with, "What the hell?!"

"Looks like she had it in for the entire town. A running list of crimes," Will commented grimly. "No one was safe."

"Which means a lot of potential suspects for murder, if we believe her note," I said.

The door to Meemaw's armoire, which Will had recently helped move down from the attic, suddenly banged. Orphie jumped back, staring, and Josie yelped then blurted, "What was that?"

Still perched on her hip, Molly squealed and clapped her pudgy hands together.

"Just the breeze," I said absently, my mind on the list. "Can I see that?" I asked Will, holding out my hand.

He caught my eye, his gaze flicking to the armoire, as he handed it over.

Orphie slammed her hands on her narrow hips and leveled her gaze at me. "Harlow Cassidy, there is no breeze inside this house. And I haven't forgotten what happened the other day... and apparently what happened to you a little bit ago."

Josie swung her head to look at Orphie, then me. "What happened the other day?" she asked.

"Yeah, what happened?" Will piggybacked.

"I...um..." I stuttered to a stop, no idea how to say that Loretta Mae had taken control of Orphie's body, just as she'd done with me minutes ago.

"Let me tell you what I think," she said, eyes flashing mischievously as if she'd figured out where I'd hidden her cookies, but she was still willing to share them with me. "First, I want you to know that I didn't used to believe in ghosts."

Josie drew her head back, giving herself a double chin. "But now you do?"

"Oh yeah, now I definitely do. I was host to one the other day...and Harlow was host to one just now."

Will arched a brow, puzzlement written on his face. I hadn't had a chance to tell him what had happened to Orphie and he'd only seen the aftermath of what had happened to me. Still, it didn't take him long to put it together and see that one plus one equaled Meemaw. "Host? As in possession?"

"Not like demons," I said quickly. "Just to...communicate."

Josie backed up, bumping up against the settee. "What are y'all talking about?" she said as she sat Molly down on the floor in front of her, handing her another toy from the diaper bag to stick in her mouth and gum.

"Meemaw," I said, at the same time Orphie said, "Harlow's great-grandmother," and Will said, "Loretta Mae."

Josie looked at each of us in turn. "What about her?"

I opened my mouth to explain, but Meemaw beat me to it. The pages of one of the magazines sitting on the coffee table rustled, flipping back and forth before suddenly stopping. Josie gasped and Orphie dropped to her knees to watch. "One of the words!" she exclaimed and pointed. "It's practically jumping off the page!"

"What word...? Oh! *I*," Josie said, seeing it for herself.

The pages flipped again, then stopped. "*Am*," Orphie read, pointing, then looking at Josie. "Do you see it?"

Josie nodded, slack-jawed.

Once again, the magazine pages flew, finally settling on yet another new page. This time Josie identified the word. "*Here.*"

"*I am here.*" Orphie looked at me.

"Okay, wait," Josie said. "Is this a Halloween trick? How'd you make the pages turn?"

"It's not a trick," Orphie said to her before turning back to me. "Am I right? It *is* your great-grandmother? She's here?"

Josie drew in a sharp breath and pressed one hand to her forehead. "What are you talking about?"

Orphie gestured one hand up and down her body. "She, like, bumped into me—"

Josie gaped, bug-eyed. "She's...um...dead," she said, her

tone making it clear she thought we might all be losing our marbles.

"She is." I gulped. "But she's also *here*."

"What, like a ghost?"

I nodded to both Josie and Orphie. "Not *like* a ghost. An *actual* ghost."

Orphie sat back on her heels. "She bumped into me and then for a few seconds? Maybe a minute? It was like I was sort of shoved aside and she was *there*." She turned to me. "That's what just happened to you, right?"

I closed my eyes for a beat and slowly nodded. "That describes it pretty well. I was still there, but she was, too. Trying to communicate."

Josie pressed her hands to her ears, squeezed her eyes shut, and wobbled her head as if she were trying to dislodge something stuck in a crevice. After a deep breath and labored exhalation, she leveled her gaze at us. "Are you actually telling me that Loretta Mae is a ghost living in this house and that she took over your bodies?"

"Shared our bodies," I corrected.

A disbelieving laugh escaped her mouth. "*Okaaay.* But you're saying the rest is true? She's a ghost? Living here? And she was *in* your bodies?"

The door to the armoire squeaked open, sounding like a labored, "*Yeeesss*," then banged closed again, punctuating the screechy sound like an exclamation point.

Will moved beside me, hands deep in his jeans pockets. "Inside you? Seriously?"

I nodded. "She was trying to communicate." What I didn't say was that the air had been rippling behind Molly, and I'd moved to create a barrier between the baby and my ghostly great-grandmother. The idea of Meemaw taking over a baby's body and making her talk was far too creepy to even contemplate. If this was something Loretta Mae was going to try again, we'd have to set some boundaries. Namely: No Children.

Orphie looked at me, her eyes strained. "I've heard the rumors. Plus, you know, your mom is Gavin's stepmom now. He doesn't know yet, but he will before long. He's seen plenty. I think he's sort of in denial."

My temple burned from the sudden sizzle where my blond hair sprouted. "What has Gavin seen?" I asked, my voice scarcely more than a whisper.

"Your mom's green thumb. Your grandmother and her goats. About Loretta Mae getting what she wants." She blinked. Looked at me hard. "And you, Harlow. About your... your Cassidy charm."

"I don't--"

"You don't need to hide it from everyone, Harlow."

I didn't. My world had grown since coming back to Bliss. Zinnia James. Sandra and Libby Allen. Will's ex-wife Naomi, and Gracie. And Madelyn Brighton. And Will. More and more people were learning the truth—or part of it—but my closest friends had been in the dark until just now. The warmth drained from my face, a chill sweeping through me. My knees went weak and, as if he sensed it, Will's hand touched the small of my back infusing me with his strength.

Josie's hands cupped her face. Her lips were parted, but she couldn't speak. For a moment, I couldn't either. The armoire door squeaked open again, then banged shut, jerking me out of my trance. I blinked. Swallowed. Orphie knew the whole truth. Now Josie did, too.

It took a long spell before Orphie, Josie, and even Will processed Meemaw's latest effort to connect with the living, and for Orphie and Josie to grasp the breadth of the Cassidy magic. The ghosts in the Cassidy closet, and the charms Butch Cassidy's Argentinian wish bestowed on all his female descendants, were not so secret anymore. And Loretta Mae, on the other side of the veil, had gone rogue.

Finally, I couldn't talk about it anymore. I made an abrupt change of subject. "So, what do we do with this ledger? And the note?" I asked the three of them, hands on my hips.

Will answered without a moment's hesitation. "Josie has to turn it over to Gavin or Hoss."

"Right," I said. "Gavin or Hoss. Gavin or Hoss." I didn't know which was the better option. "One of them needs to know."

Josie's eyes bugged and she slammed an open palm against her chest. "Me? Why do *I* have to be the one to turn it over?"

"You found it, right?" Will said. A statement, not a question.

She pulled a face but nodded. "It was in the bushes next to the porch."

"He's going to ask why you didn't bring it to him right away," Will said.

"He, who?" she asked, going pale.

"He, Gavin. Orphie's name is there. He needs to know."

"How'd it end up there?" I asked, my mind spinning with the puzzle of it all. Surely Jaclyn hadn't had it at the party. I tried to remember if any of the dancing zombies had been holding anything other than a drink. I didn't think so, but their clothes were bulky and layered, so who knew?

"I went out to clean up...some people dropped their cups over the railing." She signed, shaking her head in disappointment at how barbarian people could be. "And there it was."

Had Jaclyn put it there on purpose? Had she suspected something was going to happen to her? Had she dropped it to hide it?

"My name is in there!" Orphie screeched. "You can't turn it over to...to...to Gavin!" She buried her face in her hands.

"Oh my God, he's going to think I'm a crazy person. First the stolen LookBook and now this?"

"No he's not," I said, "and we can't cover it up. The killer's name might be in it. And Gavin is going to want to protect you and get to the truth."

After a few minutes of convincing, she dug her phone from her back pocket and dialed Gavin with trembling hands. "Baby? I...um...there's something—"

She stopped, her voice shaking, the words dying on her tongue. I took the phone from her and held it to my ear. "Gavin? It's Harlow. Orphie's here, along with Josie and Will. Josie found something you need to see."

He didn't ask any questions. Smart man. "On my way," he said.

Chapter Nine

By the time Gavin arrived, we'd migrated back to the kitchen with its butter yellow cabinets and vintage-looking appliances, a jack-o-lantern sitting on the counter next to a pile of apples. Because there was nothing better than warm apple pie on a cool autumn night.

Josie had nursed Molly before laying her on a little pallet I made out of a few blankets. In minutes, the baby was asleep. As babies went, she was easy.

A few minutes later, the bell on the front door jingled and Gavin sauntered in like a cowboy on the range, ready to wrangle and subdue whatever got in his way. The second he looked at Orphie, though, his swagger evaporated, replaced by something I'd never seen on the guy—outright *concern*. He rushed past me, Will, Josie, and little Molly cooing softly in her sleep. When he got to Orphie, who perched on the edge of one of the kitchen tables, elbows on her knees, face in hands, she looked up at him and her face crumpled.

Gavin, acting like her knight in shining armor, rushed to her. He fell to his knees and slid the last few feet, gently placing his hands on her hips. "Baby, what's wrong?"

Without a word, she put a flat palm on the journal and slid it to the edge of the table.

He glanced at it, then back at her. "What is it?"

When Orphie didn't answer, I did. "It's Jaclyn Padeski's journal."

"I found it in the shrubs by the porch," Josie said.

Gavin rocked back on his heels and stood, moving one hand to Orphie's shoulder. Damn him, when he showed such compassion for one of my best friends, it was awfully hard to keep up my dislike for him. Slowly, he was winning me over.

He pointed to the journal with his other hand. "That belonged to the deceased? And she had it at the party?"

Josie shrugged. I thought again about the zombies and I really didn't think any of them could have been carrying it. Plus Jaclyn had died at the party, so she couldn't have brought it and gotten back to the shrubs before she'd been killed...if that's what happened to her. "I don't think so," I said, "but a bunch of us were at the house helping with the setup for the party the day before. She was there. She could have brought it then? Accidentally dropped it, maybe?"

Josie snapped her fingers. "Right!" she exclaimed. Molly jerked and lifted her head, her eyelids fluttering open. Josie hurried over and rubbed her back, cooing in a soft singsong voice until the baby settled down again.

"Did she have it at your house that day?" Gavin asked, making notes on a page in the little notebook he'd fished from his jacket pocket.

Josie stood and came back to the little group. "I don't know." She frowned, but a second later her eyes went wide and she snapped again. "Wai—" she started to exclaim but caught herself and covered her mouth. We all swung our gazes to Molly, who stayed blissfully asleep. "I don't know if she had it with her, but she and Madison set up the bobbing for apples table. So maybe?" She looked at me. "That was before you got there."

Madison, who was also listed as a person to add to the ledger. Had they had a conversation? Had Jaclyn confronted her about the blackmail? Or had she dropped the book so Madison wouldn't see it and ask questions?

"So she was on the porch," Gavin said. As he slowly turned the pages of Jaclyn's notebook, I pulled out my phone and scanned through the pictures I'd taken. My gaze hitched on a different set of names, all of them smudged. It looked as if the page had gotten wet and the ink had run. It took a few seconds, but the letters on one of the lines slowly began to form into a name. The moment it did, a clanky bell rang in my mind because the name was familiar. It was one we'd talked about at Josie's house just a day before Jaclyn died.

Templeton.

Carrie Templeton.

I stared at the image on my phone. My skin erupted in goosebumps. I traced across the line with her name. A terrible thought crossed my mind. A terrible, dark scenario. What if the accident that had taken Carrie Templeton's life hadn't been an accident at all, just like Jaclyn suggested? What if Carrie Templeton had been murdered? Two pixelated scenarios came into focus, none of them featuring any of the other people who'd been at Josie's party. If Jaclyn was blackmailing her client over something—*was* she even a client or had that been a lie?—Carrie could have driven herself off the cliff—guilt and despair were powerful emotions that messed with the mind. But what if a person on Jaclyn's list didn't pay up? Could she have taken matters into her own hands? Maybe her threat was: *Pay up or you're dead!*

Until we knew if Jaclyn had something over Carrie Templeton, there was no way to know if that course of events was realistic. The big problem with trying to connect Jaclyn's death to Carrie Templeton was that Carrie Templeton was also dead. *She* couldn't have killed Jaclyn. So maybe it was a moot point.

But someone else in Jaclyn's ledger—another of her victims—very well might have killed her. That thought brought me back to Rowena Adams, Abby Lassiter, and Madison Blackstone, but I quickly shoved those names aside. My last interaction with Jaclyn played in my head. After talking about Carrie Templeton, she'd gotten agitated and launched into a tirade about how some people deserved to die. Then she'd told the story of a sleazy publisher. "Wait a second," I said, a new idea formulating.

Orphie looked up as she sniffled. "What?"

"Remember Jaclyn told us about a client suing her publisher? Do you know who it was?" I asked Josie.

Josie frowned. "No idea. She said him, though, so it was a man."

I quickly filled Will and Gavin in on the story Jaclyn had told, then continued. "He might be in the book, right? If he acted badly, which from what she said she definitely thought he did, then she might have tried to blackmail him."

"Okay," Will said, his eyebrows pulled into a V as he tried to puzzle out where my train of thought had taken me. "If you're thinking motive, that gives Jaclyn a reason to kill him— her warped sense of justice, right?"

"And it gives him motive if she *was* trying to blackmail him," I said.

Something about that conversation—or really, the way she talked about that lawsuit—made my skin prickle. "Remember when Abby's boyfriend said that thing about bouncing checks?"

"Yeah," Josie said. "That it's illegal in Texas."

"Right. But Jaclyn said it didn't matter anymore. That it was over." A tremor wound through me, reaching all the way to my temple. I pressed against it to make the electricity there stop pulsing. Will watched me, concern written on his face. The spot where that stripe of hair grew usually only tingled when I was trying to imagine someone's perfect garment. Lately, though, it had been reacting to other situations. Situations having to do with murder.

And more and more, I believed my charm had just as much to do with that dark deed and detecting as it did with sewing. I raced from the kitchen, passed Molly still sound asleep on her little pallet of quilts, and took the stairs two at a time. A gust of air filled the stairwell like wind through a tunnel. It lifted me, just slightly, speeding me along. Meemaw! That was a new trick. I returned to the kitchen a minute later with my thin rose gold laptop.

"Harlow, what are you doing?" Gavin asked as I brought the computer to life.

"The lawsuit," I said, typing into the search bar. The four of them gathered behind me, Gavin next to Orphie. He'd hardly left her side since he arrived. Will pulled up a chair and sat next to me, while Josie stayed behind my shoulder. First I searched small publishers in Texas. Publishers Archive website came up. It listed genres the various publishers specialized in: Young Adult, Children's, Mystery, Science Fiction and Fantasy, and Romance. LGBTQ+ and Nonfiction. I scrolled through the list that populated on the site and my heart sank. There had to be at least a hundred of them. But then I read the list of genres again. Children's. "Jaclyn said her client had published a children's book, right?"

I'd directed my question to Josie and she nodded. "Definitely a children's book."

I entered Children into the search box and pressed ENTER. A new page popped up, but instead of culling down the list of publishers from the first page, the search generated a slew of other content on the website with the keywords: Children and

83

Publisher. This was going to get us nowhere fast, but before I became totally dejected, another idea came to me. I opened a new tab on my laptop and entered a new search: Children's book authors in Bliss, Texas.

As it turned out, there was only one. "Patricia Baxter," I said at the same time Gavin said, "Try Patricia Baxter."

I smiled at him. I was half pleased—after all, great minds, and all that. But I was also half perplexed that Gavin and I seemed to be working together instead of him being at odds with me. I let that thought go and pulled up the county website, following the links to the judicial system page, and then to the case files search page. There I had the option to search online by name, case number, citation, or attorney. All I had was a name, so I went with that. First name: Patricia. Last name: Baxter.

I pressed the search button. A split second later, there it was with its own clickable case number. I hovered my mouse over the number, tapped my trackpad, and voila! All the information I needed was right there on my screen. "Bingo!" I exclaimed, pointing to my screen as if they weren't all huddled around me seeing it with their own eyes.

"Good thinking, Cassidy," Will said, giving my shoulder a light squeeze.

Under the STYLED section, the plaintiff and defendant were named: PATRICIA BAXTER VS. FREDERICK PRESS, LLC, BARTHOLOMEW BOLINARY. Next was the filing date. Under TYPE it said Small Claims, and under STATUS it said 'DISPOSED'. Finally, there was the judge's name.

"Disposed?" I said. "Meaning what? The case was dropped?"

"No. It means the court awarded a judgment," Gavin said. "Case closed."

The tone of his voice changed, but I didn't stop to ponder why.

"And Patricia Baxter lost," Josie said.

I immediately opened my phone's photos, then changed my mind, finding the photos icon on my desktop and opening them that way. The pictures I'd taken of the lists in Jaclyn's ledger had automatically synced to the computer. I scanned them. Bartholomew Bolinary's name didn't jump out at me, but it had been a cursory look. I zoomed in on the photo and slowed down, registering each name. Halfway down the second page of the ledger, which was the second photo I'd taken, I stopped cold. There it was. Bart Bolinary. In the second column, Jaclyn had written: *Thief* and *Lack of Ethics.* Well, that was vague. She put $10,000 in the money column, and the final column was blank.

So Bart Bolinary had not paid.

"Guess blackmail doesn't always work," Orphie said, her sniffles gone.

Will's words from a few minutes ago resurfaced. Bart Bolinary didn't have a motive to kill Jaclyn based on the lawsuit he'd won. But he certainly did if she was blackmailing him, which from his name in her ledger, she was. "Or maybe it doesn't work the way the blackmailer planned," I said.

I opened a new tab in my browser and typed in BART BOLINARY, FREDERICK PRESS, LLC, then let the search engine work its magic. A second later, a list of results appeared on my laptop screen.

I jumped and spun around at the sound of a pop. Gavin slapped his hands together as he stared at the computer. "I *knew* that name was familiar."

"He's dead," Will said.

I turned back. At the top of the search results was an article from Bliss's little local newspaper dated six months ago.

· · ·

Bart Bolinary, founder of Frederick Press, a small local publisher, dead at age 53.

I stared. And gulped. So Bart Bolinary couldn't have killed Jaclyn because he was already dead. Had Jaclyn had something to do with it? Based on her own record-keeping, the guy hadn't paid her. Had she then turned around and acted as judge, jury, and executioner?

Oh Lordy. Jaclyn Padeski had been one diabolical woman and she'd made herself a slew of enemies.

Chapter Ten

No matter how many garments I hemmed, or how many designs I sketched in my notebook, the image of Jaclyn Pandeski dressed as a zombie and laid out on Josie's side porch kept invading my thoughts. Who had she angered enough to propel someone to murder? The list seemed endless.

In my mind, I'd eliminated several people from the night of the party right out of the gate. Josie and Nate were penciled in Jaclyn's notebook, but neither were on my mental list of suspects because 1) they were dancing in her living room when Jaclyn died, and 2) they literally had no motive. They might not have been *friends* with Jaclyn, but they'd been friendly as *neighbors*. Juletta, because while she'd been at Josie's house the day before, she didn't come to the party and she had no connection to the dead woman.

I also eliminated Holly, Libby, Gracie, and Will. And myself, of course. I'd learned early on that everyone had secrets...including the Cassidy women. From the number of names in Jaclyn's ledger—and the amount of money she'd collected—it looked as if a ton of folks from Bliss had secrets they'd rather keep hidden away, too.

I reviewed the names from Jaclyn's blackmail list, trying not to think about Orphie's name there. Only three other names jumped out at me:

ROWENA ADAMS
ABBY LASSITER
MADISON BLACKSTONE

All three women had been at the Halloween party. Jaclyn hadn't gotten to adding them to her actual ledger. Did they even know they were going to be targeted for blackmail? If not, that weakened their potential motive. But if they *did* know, it made the motive very strong.

I went back to Bart Bolinary. Even if Jaclyn had been involved in his death—and knowing more about her character made it seem possible—he couldn't have been involved in her death. He didn't have the Cassidy charm so he wasn't a ghost like Loretta Mae. Thank God. A world full of all kinds of otherworldly beings floating around was a little too much to process.

Bart Bolinary was already dead, as was Carrie Templeton, who didn't appear to have been blackmailed. Was she the victim of a different crime? Had Jaclyn tried to make things right on her behalf? Exact a little revenge? But on whom?

I grabbed my cell phone, only pausing for a split second. There was only one person to call, and as much as it chagrinned me to do it, I had no choice.

Well, I *did* have a choice. I didn't *have* to get involved. But I couldn't help myself.

I dialed.

"Twice in two days," Gavin said when he answered.

"Aren't you lucky," I retorted.

"If you're calling about Jaclyn Padeski, then I probably am."

I sputtered. Leaned back against the kitchen counter. Gavin wasn't put upon by my call? He wasn't aggravated, shoving his cowboy hat back so he could scrub his face in frustration? And had he actually sort of complimented me? Had the world gone topsy-turvy?

"Speechless, I see," he commented wryly.

"I *am*, actually. Are you saying you want to hear what I have to say?"

There was a long pause—long enough for Thelma Louise to use her nose to nudge open the Dutch door that led from my kitchen to the backyard where the queen of Nana's Sundance Kids ran free. She was like Butch Cassidy himself, always evading capture, never one to be tied down.

Before I could say, *"Boo!"*, she slipped inside, her hooves clicking against the floor, and she snatched an apple from the counter. "Hey!" I hollered, lunging for her.

She stopped long enough to look at me with her crazy eyes. The horizontal, elongated pupils took in the entire room, I was sure, but I also knew she was focused on me, taunting me. As I moved toward her, she tilted her head, her pupils rotated, remaining horizontal.

And then, in a flash, she was out the door and bounding down the back steps. It's like she knew I was on the phone and wasn't likely to follow her.

"Harlow."

Gavin barking my name brought me back to the phone. "Sorry," I said. "Rogue goat."

He chuckled. "That Thelma Louise, she has a mind of her own."

I pulled the phone from my ear and stared at it. Now he was laughing and making conversation about my grandmother's goat?

"Are you okay, Gavin?" I asked, thinking that if we were in the same room, I'd be putting the back of my hand against his forehead, checking for fever.

"Peachy," he said, more sarcasm than sincerity, but that was his way. He saved whatever genuineness he had buried deep inside him for Orphie.

"Okay, listen," I said, wanting to cut to the chase. "Were you able to see anything more in Jaclyn's notebook…the line with Carrie Templeton's name?"

I heard some paper rustling over the phone line. "We've tried to enhance it, but the ink is too splotched."

I heaved a disappointed sigh, as much about the lack of clues in Jaclyn's notebook as about this collaborative conversation I was having with Gavin. It had me puzzled, as did the tenseness I detected in his voice, but I ignored the feeling as he carried on. "We've started working with Josie on who was at the party so we can cross-reference with the blackmail victims."

That was smart. "Anything yet?"

"About ten of the people at the Kincaid house that night were listed in Jaclyn's book. That leaves the possibilities pretty wide open."

"Have you ruled anyone out?" I asked.

"A handful, yup, but not most of the people helping set up for the party."

"Rowena Adams, Abby Lassiter, and Madison Blackwell," I murmured.

"You got it. The young girls are clear—Holly, the Allen girl, the baby, and Will's girl. Josie's clear. And Nate. You since your name isn't even mentioned. No connection to your friend Juletta." He trailed off and suddenly I knew why he sounded on edge—and probably why he was being so forthcoming with me. He'd left one name unspoken because he hadn't been able to exclude it and he knew I cared just as much as he did.

My friend. The love of his life. Orphie Cates.

Chapter Eleven

Will had stopped by in between meetings, something he didn't normally do unless I asked him to or we had plans. You never knew when a woman might be here trying on an outfit I'd made for her, or if I'd be measuring someone for a new design. He thought it better not to barge in. Today was an exception. "Date night?" he asked, a little twinkle in his eyes.

Date night sounded like the perfect way to distract me from Jaclyn Padeski's murder and Orphie Cates's name floating around like an anchor, pulling her down into the depths of despair. "Definitely. What do you have in mind?"

One of his eyebrows lifted mischievously. "Hmmm, a little dress up?"

"And just what kind of dress up did you have in mind?" I asked with a coy little smile.

Now his mouth twisted wryly. "How about a reprisal as Wednesday Addams?"

I tapped the pad of my finger against my lips demurely, but my eyes flashed. "Only if you'll be my Xavier."

"That's the plan," he said with a wink.

"And where are we going dressed up in our finest Halloween outfits?"

"Ahh, well, much to Gracie's dismay, I signed up at the beginning of the school year to chaperone the Halloween dance at school."

My eyes opened wider and I dipped my chin in a surprised nod. "Did you now?"

"I did. I forgot until they called to remind me."

"And you need to go in costume?"

His mouth pulled to one side. "I do."

"And you're allowed to bring a date?"

"As long as you've been fingerprinted and they've run a background check."

Which I was and they had. I'd made a slew of homecoming dresses the year before and I had desperately wanted to see the dresses and massive Texas mums in the wild. But gone were the days when you could just show up on a school campus. I'd had to go through the independent school district's rigamarole, which included fingerprints and a background check, both of which revealed nothing dodgy. I did have skeletons in my closet, but none of them had to do with criminal activity. "All good there. And lucky for you I don't have any other plans." I gave a small shrug and channeled Wednesday. "Other than reaching into the black maw of death to contact a relative, but that can wait."

"If you're sure," he said with mock concern. "I know how you value family."

Which I actually really did. Mama. Nana. Loretta Mae, even in her spectral state. I summoned up another Wednesday Addams quote. "Every day is all about me," I deadpanned, "except when it's about my family. Or you. Or designing couture..."

I trailed off and he waggled his brows. "I know. I'll pick you up at seven," he said, then gave me a lingering kiss. At the front door, he turned. "We need to set the wedding date, Cassidy."

He was right, we did. I'd wanted to put a little time and distance between Mama and Hoss's wedding. Even though that didn't work out quite the way we'd planned, they'd managed to get hitched and the celebration was still fresh for a lot of people. "It's our wedding, not your mother's," Will said, as if he'd read my mind.

I folded my arms over my chest and stared at him. "How do you do that?"

"Darlin', I know the way you think. Tessa and Hoss tied the knot. It's the wedding that wasn't. But we are going to have the wedding that is."

A shot of air suddenly spun around me like a gathering cyclone. It cannonballed up, rattling the old-fashioned milk bottle chandelier hanging in the atelier, then circled around Will. It was a streak, falling somewhere between translucent and opaque.

"I hear you, Loretta Mae," Will said. "Soon. It'll happen soon."

My great-grandmother's charm was that whatever she wanted, she got. I'd seen it in action over and over throughout my childhood. If she wanted a parking spot at the church tag sale, there was one there waiting for her. When she fancied fresh blueberries in January, a bush grew right outside the front door. I'd even seen her wish the gray right out of her hair. Her final wish, though, had been about me and Will. She'd orchestrated it so that we'd meet, hiring him to do odd tasks around the house. He wasn't a handyman, but she'd wanted it and so he'd agreed.

And she'd wanted us to fall in love.

"What if it's just her wish that made it happen?" I'd asked Will more than once and wondered more than a dozen times.

Was our love real, or was it simply the desire of a magical charm stemming from my outlaw ancestor?

Of course, he couldn't answer definitively, but he was ninety-nine percent sure that while her wish might have brought us together, it certainly couldn't make a person do something they didn't want to do.

That was true. There were boundaries and parameters to her charm, and that was one of them. A person couldn't act outside of their character or against their will—and Meemaw had known that.

Hence, I thought, her extreme joy that her scheme to get us together in physical proximity had resulted in us getting together in love. Her wish, after all, had come true.

"We'll pick a date as soon as Orphie's name is cleared, how about that?" Because there wasn't a chance in hell that I could focus on my own happy nuptials while one of my best friends was fretting over a near miss at blackmail and her name connected to a murder.

Will left and I went back to the task at hand, namely stitching the final seams on a miniature lion costume for an infant. I'd made a tiny footed sleeper and had looped yards and yards of thin satin ribbons in a muted golden hue to make the lion's mane and the fringe on the end of the stuffed tail. I worked my fingers through the mane and over each seam, clipping any wayward threads. Once it was finished, I steamed it, then folded it, wrapping it in lavender tissue paper which I taped at the center with a Buttons & Bows sticker. I put the bundle in a brown gift bag, also adorned with a sticker, and set it on the sideboard at the entry next to the other completed projects I needed to deliver or that were being picked up by excited mothers who couldn't wait to see their littles in handmade costumes.

"Date night, eh?" Juletta appeared in the atelier. She'd figured out how to come into the shop without rattling the bells on the door. When I'd asked her how long she was staying—now that she'd made amends with Orphie—she'd shrugged noncommittally. "I've never been to Texas. I'm just exploring, so a while longer."

Keeping Meemaw at bay when Juletta was around was a full-time job. I saw the ripple of air behind Juletta and I jumped up, grabbing her arm and pulling her toward the kitchen. "Yes! Wearing our costumes again."

She pulled her arm from my grip and pulled an astonished face. "What's going on?"

"What? Nothing," I said, sounding far too innocent.

Juletta eyes me suspiciously. "I'll be upstairs," she said.

The second I heard the soft click of the guest room door closing, I wheeled around, searching for Meemaw. "Don't you dare," I warned her. She needed to say no to possessing another person's body. "Do you understand?"

The pipes clanged and I took that as yes.

As I went on to the last project for the day, my thoughts spiraled around Rowena Adams, the young librarian, who definitely looked the part of someone who had a dark side. Had Rowena known Carrie? I made a mental note to visit the library where Rowena worked. Maybe I could catch a fly with some honey.

And then there were Madison Blackstone and Abby Lassiter. Madison was a teacher. Her name, like Abby's, Rowena's, and Orphie's, had been penciled in, not yet added to the *actual* blackmail list. Could any of them have figured out what Jaclyn was up to? I'd studied my copy of the ledger. Next to Abby's name, it said *association* but crossed out. Rowena and Madison had a dollar amount listed, and Madison had DUI.

Once my mind glommed onto a train of thought, I couldn't chase it away. It was just two o'clock. Plenty of time to dig into one of them to see what I could find out. The earsplitting ring of my cellphone snapped me back to the moment. Orphie. It played the mysterious ringtone I'd chosen for her, what I imagined she might walk on the catwalk to. "Hey," I said when I answered. "How are you fee—"

Her panicked voice cut me off. "I'm at the sheriff's office!"

So she'd gone to see Gavin. "Do they know something?" I asked.

"Harlow!" She yelled, her banshee voice erupting through the speaker of my cell phone, practically shattering my eardrums.

"What?!" I hollered back, mirroring her volume and pitch, which was a solid octave higher than my usual tone.

Then she sobbed and an invisible knife impaled my heart with the first thought that came to mind and I knew what she was going to say before she said it. "They brought me in for questioning," she cried.

The pit of my stomach dropped. No. No, no, no. My body felt like a raging volcano ready to blow and hurl molten lava all over my atelier and Buttons & Bows. I seethed red, muttering under my breath. "Gavin McClaine, you son of a— "

I could almost hear her shaking her head as she blurted, "No! It's not him. He was *with* me when they came and he was so angry. They kept it from him because we're...we're..."

Enough said. I wondered if he'd had an inkling when we'd spoken, or if he was truly in the dark. The next possibility chilled my blood even more. Surely not my step-daddy. "Who then? Hoss?"

"No. A different deputy. A woman." Orphie drew in a shaky breath. "And she is *not* nice, either."

My plans for finding Abby, visiting Rowena at the library or calling Madison flew out of my head. Only helping Orphie remained, my determination going from zero to a hundred in as long as it took me to mute the call and yell, "Meemaw!" I needed her strength right now.

A faint buzzing sound grew louder and a second later, that faint form that had been like a tornado when Will had been here was back. Instantly, I felt settled. My heartbeat slowed. I could do this. I could help Orphie. I unmuted. "Did they arrest you?" I asked. I pressed Speaker and set the phone down long enough to slip on a burnt orange jacket I'd made to take me through the autumn months. People around here thought I'd done it in honor of UT Austin's colors, but really it was just a nod to the few trees that actually changed from green to a cornucopia of reds, oranges, and yellows.

"No. I mean, not yet. How can they think I had anything to do with this?" she wailed. "I didn't even know her!"

That was a great question.

When she spoke again, her voice was a smidgeon calmer... or at least the edge of the shrillness was gone. "Harlow, *please*. You have to find out what happened."

I stopped, absorbing her request. I had been involved in solving a few recent crimes and I'd begun to wonder if that wasn't actually part of my Cassidy charm, too. Sewing. Death. Detecting. Whatever. It didn't matter at this moment in time. I would move mountains to help Orphie. I paused for a second to slow my mind down. I needed to think, not just react. Deep breathe in, slowly release. Deep breathe in, slowly release. After the third one, I launched myself into action. I snatched up the phone and the keys to Buttercup, scratched Earl Gray's ears, wagged a finger at nothing in particular, hoping Meemaw saw it and understood to steer clear of Juletta, and then I bolted out the front door. Down the porch steps. Across the yard. Through the gate. Then I practically threw myself into the truck. "I'm on my way. Sit tight," I said.

Orphie barked out a laugh. "Do I have any other choice?"

No, in fact, she did not. I jabbed my finger on the End

Call button and navigated to my favorites. I didn't have Hoss's number saved there, but Mama's was at the top. I pressed the flat button and dialed. She answered before the first ring had finished. "I've been expectin' your call, Peach."

"I bet you have, Mama. Now where is he?"

"Oh no. You're not talkin' to my husband all fired up like you are."

"Right now he's the sheriff, Mama, not your husband."

"Oh come now. We're hitched. He's always my husband. And Harlow Jane Cassidy, you need to simmer down. He's doin' his job, that's all."

That's all? That's all! "No that is *not* all. He hauled Orphie to the station, Mama. Orphie! For murder! And you know that she is the farthest...the *farthest*...thing from a murderer that can possibly exist." It was true. She was peaches and cream. She was ribbons and bows and butterflies. Like Josie, Orphie saw the good in everyone. She stopped to move a snail or frog or worm off the sidewalk and back to safety, was all about relocating snakes—even deadly copperheads—which frankly I didn't understand. She wouldn't kill someone and she owned up to her mistakes.

"All I know is that the deputy had enough to bring her in for questioning. Hoss didn't wanna do it, but Harlow, you know he has to do his job."

"Orphie said that deputy is *not* nice!" I said for no particular reason.

"I reckon Orphie wants you to help prove her innocence," Mama said. A statement, not a question.

"Yes, she does. And I'm going to do it, too."

"Now darlin', think about it. Why do you suppose Hoss gave her a phone call right away? And he let her call you?"

"I've seen all the crime shows. She gets a phone call. They can't deny her that. Also, she's not actually arrested."

"True, but he made it happen the second she walked into the station. Before they even talked to her—"

"You mean interrogated her—"

"Harlow, Hoss doesn't believe Orphie is guilty any more than you or I do. But he has to do his job."

I felt steam building in my head, ready to spew from my ears like a cartoon character. "Well, Mama," I said, "what you and I think doesn't matter right now, does it?"

"Harlow Jane Cassidy," she said again, but I had other fish to fry. "Gotta go spring my friend from the pokey," I said.

"Wait—" she started, but I jammed my finger on the End button and the line went dead.

I yanked the steering wheel to the left, leaving the downtown square and rumbling toward the sheriff's station. "Call Gavin McClaine," I said to my phone. Like Mama, he answered on the first ring, and like before, he launched into the middle of a conversation we hadn't been having. "I'm working on it, Harlow. I've got a call in to Brendan Phillips—"

"Who's that? A lawyer? Will he get her out of there?"

"Yes, and yes."

"What happened, Gavin?" I demanded.

"They're keepin' me out of the loop because we're... we're..."

He hesitated just like Orphie had so I filled in the blank. "What? Because you're a couple. I get it, but still—"

"Because we're married, Harlow."

I jerked the car off the road and slammed my foot on the brake. In my head, I screamed the words, but they came out cool and controlled. "I'm sorry, what did you say?"

Gavin exhaled a heavy sigh. "We eloped, Harlow. The day after Josie's party. We went to Dripping Springs and we got married at the courthouse. Hoss knows. And he knows I can't be involved. He also knows he can't stop me. But at the moment, I'm completely in the dark."

Chapter Twelve

Ten minutes later, I was plowing through another door, this one leading me straight into the sheriff's station. I wanted to bellow with undeniable fierce authority, "Hoss McClaine, get your skinny behind out here, pronto!" But, of course, I couldn't say that to my brand-spanking new step-daddy. Instead, I slowed my pace and schooled my expression, trying to calm my thrashing heart. My first realization was that I didn't recognize the woman sitting at the desk behind the bulletproof barrier. Her fingertips tapped relentlessly against the keyboard of the computer she was focused on. Once I got close enough, I saw her name tag read *Deputy Shipley.* A vertical line carved its way between my brows. Was *she* the not-nice deputy who'd brought Orphie in for questioning?

I waited for her to acknowledge me, but she kept tap, tap, tapping. Finally, I cleared my throat and Deputy Shipley raised her brown eyes to me. Her long hair was braided, the plait hanging over one shoulder. Her khaki uniform was identical to the one Gavin always wore, minus the white cowboy hat. "Sorry 'bout that. What can I do for you?" she said, the words more congenial than her tone. Still, it took some of the wind out of my sails."

A vision flashed in my mind. A floral jumper with wide legs, the base color a deep, forest green. If I were to make it for Deputy Shipley, I wondered what wishes and dreams of hers might come true.

"Uh, hell*o*?"

There was the attitude I'd expected. The momentary reprieve from my anger over Orphie's arrest bubbled back up. "Yep. I need to see the sheriff," I said. As an afterthought, I forced a smile knowing it was probably too late. There would be no honey from this fly.

"You *need* to see the sheriff," Shipley repeated, her words coming out mocking and sarcastic.

"I do," I said. "I *need* to see the sheriff. Right now."

She stifled a derisive chuckle—barely. "That's not how it works."

I folded my arms and cocked my head. "Oh, I know how things work around here, believe me. And I *need* to see him."

"And just *what* do you need to see the sheriff about?" she asked, sounding like she wasn't going to believe a word I said.

"That's between me and him."

She barked out a laugh. "I'm not going to trouble Sheriff McClaine unless I know what you want to see him about," she practically spat.

I had never seen this woman before and I was probably as far from menacing as I could be in my jeans and orange jacket. My temple pulsed and buzzed like something inside me was short-circuiting, but I forced my attention away from the sensation and pressed my hands on the counter. I leaned close to the glass and glowered at her. "It's none of your business, and you *absolutely* need to trouble him. And you need to trouble him...*Right. Now.*"

Any last vestiges of pleasantness evaporated at the 'or else' implied by my words. She leveled her bark-colored eyes at me. "Oh no, no, no. You don't come in here and demand to see anyone, least of all the sheriff."

Hoss McClaine and I had been on shaky ground my whole life—or at least since my teen years, but our relationship had become more stable once he and my mother made their relationship public, and even more solid when I'd warmed up Tessa's cold feet just before they got hitched. I was pushing it right now, but if I had to pull out the familial connection to spring Orphie from the pokey, then that's exactly what I'd do. I flashed a saccharine smile and leaned in again. "Just tell my *step-daddy* that his loving step-daughter is here."

At this, Deputy Shipley blinked. Frowned. Swallowed. But she remained seated.

I met her gaze head on and without a wavering eye. "Go on. I'll wait."

A smirk curled her lips. "So *you're* Harlow Cassidy."

The way she said it sounded like it might not be a good thing in her book to be me. That probably meant Gavin had given her an earful before he'd started warming up to me. "Oh, so you know who I am. That's great," I said, trying hard to keep my feathers from getting more ruffled than they already were. "Then you know Hoss'll see me just as soon as you let him know I'm here."

"The sheriff is—"

"Right here, deputy," a gravelly voice said. "I'll take it from here."

She broke off and a visible lump slid down her throat as Sheriff Hoss McClaine sauntered up behind her. Hoss was as weathered as a man could get, the result of age and the brutal Texas sun. If you happened upon him in the street, you might think he had just ridden in on a sweaty horse after moving a herd of cattle across the Oregon Trail, or maybe he'd just wrangled a mess of outlaws. He was the spitting image of an old west lawman, complete with cowboy regalia. His full head of iron-gray hair lacked the bits of black that sliced through the salt-and-pepper mustache and the soul patch that grew just below his lower lip.

My step-daddy could have walked off the set of a Clint Eastwood Spaghetti Western and no one would have blinked an eye. He didn't smile at me, but I detected a little twinkle of amusement in his eyes at my doggedness—and at the tinge of pink on the deputy's cheeks. I'd heard him say on more than one occasion: "Authority is a funny thing." The deputy's chagrined reaction to his sudden appearance proved his point, and then some.

"This way, Harlow," he said. He opened the locked door that separated the lobby from the inner workings of the building, letting me pass through first. Ever the gentleman. He let the door close then strode past me, back the way he'd come, with me as the caboose to a two-car train.

With each step down the hallway toward Hoss's office, my agitation grew until I was a balloon stretched to capacity and ready to pop. I needed to talk to Orphie face to face. She needed to see a friend rather than all the foes she was currently surrounded by. Not to mention I wanted to ask her about her *elopement*, but I knew I'd have to bite my tongue on *that* particular subject—at least for the time being. Priorities.

Hoss led me into his office, a place I hadn't seen since my law-breaking youth. The decor hadn't changed much from my recollection. It was minimal. The only personality was a wedding photo with my mama. In it, Tessa beamed. The silver streak sprouting from above her temple almost glowed. I touched my own, pressing against the hairline again to stop the tingling I was still experiencing. It was the equivalent of Peter Parker's Spidey senses. Right now, it had grown to a mighty crackling, all due to Orphie. The closer I was to her, detained as she was, the more my hair follicles fired. "Hoss," I started, but I stopped short when he held up one hand, palm out.

"I have somethin' to say first," he said. My nod was less giving him permission and more acknowledging that he was in charge here and if he wanted to go first, I certainly couldn't stop him. "Your friend, Orphie Cates, is safe. She doesn't need one but her lawyer is on the way." He shook his head, looking momentarily flummoxed. "Those Kincaids. They jump the gun." He held out his palm to stop me from interrupting and kept talking. "I'll let you speak to her, but listen up, Harlow, I don't want you interferin' in a murder investigation, because that's what we think this is. In her own words, Jaclyn Padeski says she was murdered. Don't know how and don't know why, but we're gonna figure it out and I don't need you buttin' in."

I barely kept my mouth shut as I fidgeted and nodded along as he spoke and he barely got the last word out when I blurted, "I was there! She didn't kill anyone!"

"I don't reckon she did. She's a touch dramatic—"

"Your deputy brought her in for questioning! Why not just do that at her house?"

He ran his hand over his face, shaking his head again. "It was unnecessary, I admit. And we are just questionin' her is all. One by one, we have to make our way through our list of suspects. We're working on whittlin' down the list."

I jammed my hands on my hips and glared at him. "If she doesn't need to be here, let her go!"

"Simmer down, Harlow," he said with his best placating tone. "I'm gonna let you see her. That's a whole lot more'n I should...since she asked for a lawyer."

I dragged in a deep breath, held it to the count of four, and then blew it out with a vengeance. It didn't help. "So you're talking to everyone whose name is in Jaclyn's book?"

"We are. We also got a phone call about Orphie." He let

out a heavy sigh. "So there's that. We have no choice but to question her."

"What phone call?" I demanded.

He peered at me. "I don't recall deputizin' you, Harlow." He paused, looking mighty exasperated. "I shouldn't say any more, but here's what we have. A witness overheard an argument between the deceased and Orphie Cates at the Halloween party. This witness says that a threat was made."

My blood seemed to stop flowing for a minute. My body turned cold. "Wait, what? What witness? What argument? Where?"

As I asked the questions, I saw that figure hurrying down the sidewalk the morning Orphie and Juletta had talked. That had to have been Jaclyn Padeski, but Jaclyn was dead so she couldn't be the anonymous witness who'd come forward to throw Orphie under the bus.

"I know you and Orphie are friends," Hoss was saying. "Do I want her to be guilty? Of course, I don't. Is she a person of interest? Maybe. Do I think she did it? I'm hopin' the answer to that proves to be no."

Needles pricked the insides of my eyelids. I blinked back the tears. "Who said Orphie threatened Jaclyn?" I asked, more quietly, concern creeping into my voice.

"You know I can't tell you that, Harlow."

"She doesn't have it in her to kill anyone, Hoss."

Even beneath his furry lip, I detected the deep frown. "You know as well as I do that anyone can do any damn unexpected thing when they're pushed. But I hope you're right, Harlow. I sincerely do. Now, do you want to talk with her?"

"With her? You mean with your *daughter-in-law*," I said, and for a split second, his hard demeanor cracked. He zipped it back up and scowled. "I reckon she is that now."

"Mama *told* me you don't think Orphie did it," I said,

sounding much more like a defiant kid than I wanted to. "Mama said—"

His growl stopped me cold. "Tessa don't speak for me, Harlow, just like I don't speak for her. I'm humorin' you though, since you are my step-daughter and all. And like you said, that girl in there is now married to Gavin." He wagged his finger between us. "She's our kin. Yours and mine. Believe me, I'll do whatever I can to get her outta here quick."

Wow. He was right. Orphie was more than just my friend. She was my step-sister-in-law. She was *family*. I had my brother Red, but now Orphie was actually my *sister*.

Hoss led me into a small interview room with a table, two chairs, and a video camera mounted in the corner at the ceiling. It was just as every interview room appeared in every crime show I'd ever seen. "Have a seat. I'll go get her."

From what Hoss said, Orphie wasn't under arrest, and this wasn't a prison, so I didn't think they had a visiting area and or even kept hardened criminals here. Thank heavens for small favors. I waited, my hands nervously twining around each other. I believed Hoss when he said questioning Orphie was routine, but he was also right about Orphie's reaction. She could be a little on the dramatic side and being hauled to the sheriff's station for questioning certainly qualified as reason for drama.

When she came to the door, ushered in by Hoss, her dark hair, usually full and bouncy, was lifeless. Her normally fiery eyes were dim. And her beautiful brown skin showed not a trace of the glimmer it usually had. Orphie was a naturally bubbly personality, but all her effervescence had dissipated like soda that had gone flat. I jumped up and ran to her. As I reached her, her knees gave out. I lunged, slipping my arms under hers to try to hold her up but she hung like a rag doll. Hoss took one side and I took the other, and together, we guided her to the chair.

I pulled the other chair around the table and sat knee to knee with her, nodding thanks to Hoss. He dipped his chin in return and strode out of the room, leaving us alone. The instant the door closed, Orphie's face went slack around her red-rimmed eyes. She started to talk, but the words caught in her hoarse voice. She cleared her throat and tried again, finally choking out, "I lied to you," she said, her voice shaky.

I stared. "What?"

"When I said I didn't know Jaclyn—"

I gaped. "You did? You knew her?"

"No! B-but she came up to me at the p-party. Like she knew m-me. She said she knew I s-stole from Maximillian!" she wailed. "She really *did* want to blackmail me! But h-how c-could they think I k-killed her? I didn't! I didn't kill her!"

I suddenly remembered seeing Orphie talking with someone at the party. Her demeanor had seemed so off, like she was lost in her own world. I'd thought it was Jaclyn's death. It *was* about Jaclyn, but not about her dead body by the overturned apple barrel. It was because of the threat.

I squeezed her hand, wishing I could infuse her with reassurance but knowing I couldn't. She'd lied, and she'd upped the ante by asking for her lawyer. I came back to the phone call Hoss said they'd received. "Did someone see you talking at the party?" I asked her.

"There were people around, but everyone was in costume. Maybe someone heard? I don't know!"

"Did you tell Gavin?" I asked. "That Jaclyn spoke to you?"

She nodded as she bent at the waist, putting her head between her knees. "He's my...we got..." The muffled words faded away.

"I know," I said. "He told me."

"He said he believes me," she said as she looked up at me through her red-rimmed eyes. She squeezed my hands. "You believe me, right? I didn't do this."

I squeezed her hands right back. "I believe you. And don't you worry," I told her, ready to ignore Hoss's warning that I not interfere with the investigation. "I'm going to talk to Gavin and we'll get to the bottom of this Orphie"

Before I got up to leave, I hugged her tight. "Congratulations on the wedding, Mrs. McClaine."

"Mrs. *Cates*-McClaine," she said through watery eyes.

"Mrs. Cates-McClaine. It has a nice ring to it," I said, then I left her to wait for her lawyer.

Chapter Thirteen

As I reentered the lobby of the sheriff's station, Deputy Shipley still sat at the desk. She glanced at me, not bothering to put on a fake smile. It wasn't quite a scowl but it was darn close.

The door from outside swooshed open and a man charged in, breathless. Shipley and I reacted at the same time, her with a surprised and suddenly ultra pleasant, "Deputy McClaine!" and me with a slightly less pleasant and more accusatory, "Gavin!"

Gavin practically skidded to a stop next to me. With a dismissive nod at Shipley, he grabbed me by the arm. I hardly had a split second to process where his anger at her was coming from when he growled into my ear. "Come with me." And then he dragged me toward the door he'd just entered through.

I could have dug my feet in and resisted, but my last conversation with him had not been antagonistic like our talks normally were. We both had the shared interest of exonerating Orphie, so I propelled myself into motion and went willingly. I couldn't resist throwing a backward glance over my shoulder at Shipley. She stared, open-mouthed and in obvious consternation. It felt like confirmation of what I'd thought when I'd first laid eyes on her. I'd bet Loretta Mae's old Singer that Deputy Shipley was the not-nice one who'd actually—literally —brought Orphie in. She was *clearly* enamored with Gavin. Had she taken such an aggressive stance about Orphie in hopes of winning his heart? Oh, poor foolish woman. If she did overplay her hand with Orphie, Gavin would never forgive her.

I pulled myself to a stop, still staring at her. "You—" I started, but stumbled and let out a loud "Oomph!" as Gavin yanked me outside. I shook my arm free and jabbed a finger in the general direction of Deputy Shipley. "It was her!"

Gavin rocked back on his cowboy booted heels, angry arms folded over his chest. "That doesn't matter right now, Harlow."

I glared at Shipley through the glass, then back at Gavin. "Of course it does!"

"If I'd taken that call, it would've been me who'd had to bring her in for questioning. It doesn't matter right now," he said again.

I didn't believe that for a second. It mattered. A lot. Gavin would never have brought Orphie in for questioning. He would have talked to her, she would have told him the truth then and there, and he would have directed his attention to finding out who had overheard Jaclyn and Orphie talking at the party. Because *that* person was the guilty one.

"We need to work together," Gavin said, "because one of the people in Jaclyn Padeski's little blackmail book is making my...my..."

I blinked, then realized what he was trying to say. "Your *wife*," I said, and he bit his lower lip so hard I thought he might draw blood.

"My *wife*," he repeated, saying the word as if he was testing it out for the first time. "I haven't gotten used to that yet, and we've been keeping it on the down low. She didn't want to steal your thunder with your engagement and all."

Aw, Orphie. My heart swelled. She was keeping her own happiness under wraps to protect mine. Didn't she know that I didn't give two hoots about that? I wanted to celebrate her happiness with her, even if that happiness was now tied inextricably to Gavin McCaine.

Gavin finished the sentence he'd started, which snapped me back to the moment. "One of those people is making my wife the fall guy for a murder she most definitely did not commit."

I would have told anyone who'd listen that Gavin wanting to collaborate with me on anything—law-related or otherwise —would happen when the Cowboys left Dallas for greener pastures, i.e. never. But here he was wanting to do just that. I couldn't dwell on it though, and I didn't even want to acknowledge how shocked I was for fear he'd do a complete about-face and walk away. We'd both studied Jaclyn's journal and ledger and had come to the same conclusion. Right now, two heads seemed better than one. Even if one of those heads belonged to him.

Just as Carrie Templeton's terrible car accident had been, Jaclyn Padeski's death was front page news in Bliss's hometown newspaper. And just as Gavin had said it would, an autopsy was being done. As of now, the cause of death was unknown. But, as Hoss had said, Jaclyn's own words had them investigating the death as a murder.

That first day I saw Jaclyn Padeski in Josie's kitchen, she had talked a lot about the sleazy publisher her client had lost to in small claims court. She'd talked about murder and people getting what they deserved. And she'd absently piped icing on cookies, almost indifferent to the subject as if talking about murder was some sort of everyday topic of conversation people had all the time. *Every time someone dies, I think, what if it was murder?* she'd said.

Those words spun through my mind like a cyclone taking form in a turbulent sky. She'd brought up Carrie Templeton, although she'd called her a client. "Carrie told Jaclyn something," I said under my breath, trying the idea on for size, then louder. "Carrie Templeton told her hairdresser, Jaclyn Padeski, something."

Gavin stared at me. "What?"

I turned my back to him, pacing. Thinking. If Carrie had been on that windy two-lane road and had tried to slow down as she'd rounded a curve only to have no brakes, she would have gone straight over the edge. The theory had been that she hadn't tried to stop. That she'd plunged over the cliff on purpose. I used Jaclyn's approach of asking 'what if?' just as we'd briefly done in Josie's kitchen. What if someone had messed with the brakes? Drained the fluid? But if that was the case, first, who might have done it, and second, why?

"Gavin," I said, ready to talk it through with him. "Jaclyn said something when we were all at Josie's." He stood rooted to the ground and waited for me to continue, his expression stony. "She said that some people deserved to die."

One of his eyes twitched, just barely, but it was enough that I knew he was thinking about the layered meanings of that statement. "You're thinking vigilante justice?"

I'd already wondered if her blackmail method was *pay up or else I'll kill you*. Bart Bolinary was dead after all. That theory was starting to make more and more sense. "I mean, maybe? She was blackmailing people based on things she knew about them. Bad things they did. If she had her own misguided sense of justice, she could rationalize it, right?"

He picked up the thought and ran with it. "If someone did something really bad, then they deserved what they got. And she felt justified in executing that sentence."

"Vigilante justice on behalf of some other wronged person."

It wasn't a leap to say the anonymous caller who'd implicated Orphie in the killing of Jaclyn Padeski was probably the actual murderer and had probably overheard Jaclyn confront Orphie at the party. They were definitely trying to direct the authorities to her. That's how it worked in TV dramas, and it worked because it made the most sense. Why else would someone make up a story about overhearing the two women arguing just before Jaclyn's death?

Any case against Orphie had more holes in it than a yard of eyelet fabric. I'd sooner believe that Meemaw could *actually* come back to life, her taking possession of a living person's body notwithstanding than that Orphie had had a hand in Jaclyn's murder "Rowena said something that day. Something about six degrees of separation."

"Or to Kevin Bacon," he said.

What was it with Kevin Bacon and however many degrees of separation? "Right Only in this case, it was about Carrie Templeton."

Gavin squinted his eyes against the autumn sun. "The woman who drove off the cliff."

"Right. Rowena said we all probably knew someone who knew her. *And* her name was in Jaclyn's book—"

"Not in the blackmail column," he mused.

Right again. We hadn't been able to figure out the purpose of the smudged names, but a possible answer came to me in a flash. "They're the ones she was getting justice *for.*"

"Okay," he said, drawing out the second half of the word. "There are a lot of names in that book. Why her? Why Carrie Templeton? It was determined that was a probable suicide. There were no skid marks. She went right over the edge."

Exactly what the other women had said, and what I'd read in the online newspaper. "But what if it *was i*ntentional?" I thought about how Jaclyn had confronted Orphie, almost giving her a heads-up that something bad was coming her way. Had she done the same for whoever she thought had a hand in Carrie Templeton's death? Had that early warning been the catalyst for someone to get rid of Jaclyn before she lorded whatever she knew over them? Something wicked this way comes.

"Jaclyn was the person who brought up Carrie Templeton at Josie's house the day before the party," I continued. I explained who had been there and what we'd been doing. We were getting close to the truth, I could feel it in my bones. My breath came fast as I turned and paced the sidewalk in front of the station. I walked in a circle, then drew up short right in front of him. The implication suddenly seemed so clear. Jaclyn had been saying she *knew* Carrie's death wasn't an accident—and she was saying it to someone in that room that day at Josie's. We'd been trying to link Jaclyn's death to someone at the *Halloween* party, but what we needed to do was connect it to one of the people in Josie's kitchen the day *before* the party.

That logic led me to the same three people: Rowena, Abby, and Madison. All of them were in Jaclyn's notebook, they'd all been in the kitchen that day, they'd all been at the party, and none of them had been marked as PAID.

Orphie had *not* been at Josie's the day before the party. That in itself didn't exonerate her, but if it led to the real killer, that's all we needed.

Gavin ran his hand down his face, cupping his jaw as he considered my theory. "So we need to find out what Carrie Templeton was up to and who had something to gain by her murder.

He suddenly took off, heading back to the entrance of the sheriff's station. I didn't know what he was doing so I stayed put. At the door, he turned to look at me. "Are you coming?"

I pressed an open palm to my chest, my eyes popping open wide. "Me?"

He pulled a face. "Who else?"

Right. Who else? "Yeah, sure," I said, and hurried after him, past Deputy Shipley who frowned at us, and into the bullpen where three people sat at their desks, one intent on their laptop computer, the other two on their cellphones. It wasn't like the bustling law enforcement agencies portrayed in the media but was about a third of the size, sparse, and felt understaffed. Then again, Bliss was a small town, so maybe this—along with whoever was out in the field, plus Deputy Shipley—was more than enough people to keep it safe.

Gavin sat at his desk, which was face-to-face with another of the same size. A few seconds later, he'd pulled up a PDF of Jaclyn's notebook and printed two copies of the final pages. He retrieved them from the communal printer, and handed one of them to me, followed by a standard yellow highlighter. He kept the other copy and grabbed another highlighter for himself. He sat, then gestured to the chair sitting alongside his desk.

The surface of his workspace fell somewhere between less than tidy, but not quite messy, either. It showed that he did, in fact, work here on crime-solving. A collage-style frame held five photos of him and Orphie. He glanced at it and swallowed hard before studying the pages he held. I didn't need him to instruct me on the plan. We were looking for all the people who had been at Josie's party when Jaclyn was killed and/or hadn't paid Jaclyn despite her efforts at blackmailing them. Even if Rowena Adams, Abby Lassiter, and Madison Blackstone were the most logical leads, we still needed to eliminate anyone else.

As if he'd read my mind, Gavin said, "We need to cross our Ts and dot our Is."

We scoured our lists and three minutes later, if that, we compared our findings, which were almost identical.

The people on the list who'd been present when Jaclyn died were Rowena Adams, Abby Lassiter, and Madison Blackstone. No surprise there. No wildcard showed up. "A DUI for Madison Blackstone. Association crossed out for Abby Lassiter, whatever that means. And a question mark for Rowena Adams," I said. Drugs, maybe? That had been on Jaclyn's list of crimes.

"Welp, as the saying goes, the closest route between two places is a straight line. We know what we have to do."

I gulped, half with surprise and half with pride. We. He'd said we, like we were a bonafide crime-solving team.

Chapter Fourteen

I couldn't be rash, I decided, which meant I needed a plan. I spent the rest of the day playing catch-up on all the little jobs I was contracted for. Couture wasn't big in Bliss. That meant that lately, my bread was buttered by pants that needed hemming, dresses that needed taking in or letting out, and other menial sewing tasks. I'd just been tasked with two holiday dresses, but I worked in an orderly fashion, doing jobs in order. Skipping ahead to the more interesting or fun projects meant I'd never get to the little jobs. Discipline. Meemaw had taught me that. Mama's gift didn't require control or routine in the way I needed. I'd made a business out of my love of fibers and fashion. Mama just made flowers bloom and plants grow. For Nana, the Sundance Kids was a business, but she was lackadaisical about the things she made with goat milk. Cheese and soap could wait if something else came up that took priority in her mind. But this—my sewing and dress designing—*this* was how I made a living. I couldn't afford to let things slip. The small jobs kept me going in between the bigger but less frequent garment projects.

I made the final stitch in the hem of a pair of men's slacks, tied off the thread, and laid the pants on the ironing board. The steamer was primed and ready, and three minutes later, the creases were sharp and the stitches in the hem of each pant leg were pressed and invisible. Instead of hanging completed garments, I sometimes opted to fold and wrap them in tissue paper, affixing a Buttons & Bows sticker to hold the bundle together. The presentation made it seem like a gift to be opened.

I checked the task off my To-do list and moved on to the next items—three Luna Lovegood costumes for eleven-year-old identical triplet sisters. One would dress in the traditional black Hogwarts attire complete with a charcoal pleated wool skirt and sweater, white blouse, tie, tights, and a Hogwarts robe with a Ravenclaw emblem. One would wear Luna's goldenrod, dark peach, and rose ruffled dress, and the third would wear the eccentric character's quintessential quirky outfit with the blue tights, black skirt with a colorful pattern, rose-colored tailored jacket, and funky glasses shaped like hands, one lens rose the other blue. The girls had come in for fittings, and with their long blond hair, they'd each be the spitting image of the Harry Potter character.

The blouse, socks, and shoes were not part of the job, and I'd found a Hogwarts Ravenclaw emblem to adhere to the robe. The rest of the pieces could have been purchased online and for less money than what I was charging to make them, but the girls' mom wanted something one-of-a-kind for her daughters. Who was I to say no?

I was going to make those girls shine as Luna Lovegood.

I kept the two sides of my cutting table folded down, the whole thing pushed up against one wall of the atelier. It was on casters, making it easy to move around the room. I pulled it out and extended both sides, then laid out the black twill fabric for the robe, the black lining, and the red satin for the lining of the hood. As I inserted the last pin to hold the pattern pieces onto the fabric, my cell phone buzzed. The incoming text from Gavin appeared on the screen.

Sudden Death.

I stared at the message. What? I texted.

He texted back right away. Her blood alcohol was elevated but not high enough to kill her. Preliminary toxicology is inconclusive. Current finding is Sudden Death.

What does that mean?

Basically they don't know.

Three flashing dots appeared, then disappeared, then appeared again. Between us, Cassidy.

Scout's honor, I replied, adding a raised hand emoji. I had never been any type of Scout, and I was pretty sure Gavin knew that, but if he did or cared, he didn't say.

Officially, it's deemed Sudden Death. At this point there's no obvious cause.

Not an overdose? I texted. The zombies *had* been dancing frenetically.

Waiting for toxicology.

A few days? I asked.

A few weeks.

WEEKS!

This isn't CSI, he responded and I could almost hear the irritation. In real life it takes time.

I shuddered and tried to imagine how that could have happened. If she'd been drunk, she might have tried to bob for an apple. Had she passed out bent over the barrel, her head in the water? It happened to impaired people in bathtubs. Sinead O'Connor. Whitney Houston. Dolores O'Riordin. How ironic that the song Zombie had been playing, sung by O'Riordin, just moments before Jaclyn died in a similar fashion. All I could think was that Jaclyn had been wrong when she'd penned that note predicting foul play if anything happened to her.

They're sure she didn't drown? I typed.

Three dots appeared, then disappeared, then appeared again. Finally, words appeared on my screen. I think the medical examiner knows what she's doing.

Right. I wasn't calling out the ME for being wrong, I was just trying to come up with possibilities. Air had stopped flowing to her lungs. So how did she stop breathing? Heart attack?

Again, the three dots appeared and disappeared before his response came. That would be Sudden Cardiac Death. The ME says there's no evidence of that.

So we had to wait on toxicology to find out how Jaclyn Padeski died, and who knew how long that would take. As I headed upstairs to get ready for date night with Will at the high school Halloween dance, the constant electric charge going on at my temple underscored my unease. But maybe we didn't have to wait. If we could figure out how the killer had killed her, *that* would lead us to the truth.

Chapter Fifteen

"Don't get involved," Will said. I had my cell phone on Speaker so we could talk as I slipped into my black ruffly Wednesday Addams dress for the second time.

"I have to—"

"You don't. Let Gavin do his job, Cassidy. I'm serious. If you're right and someone you know actually killed Jaclyn, and they find out you're trying to out them, you'll be in danger. Someone who'd killed once isn't going to shy away from killing again."

He was right on all counts, and we'd had this discussion before, but I wasn't going to let his argument stop me. Orphie's freedom was on the chopping block. "I can be subtle," I said.

"Can you though?" he asked dryly.

I tied up my hair and slipped on a hairnet to keep it in place, then bent over at the waist to slip on my Wednesday wig. Standing upright, the blood rushed from my head and a wave of dizziness washed through me. I blinked, and it was gone. Looking in the mirror, I adjusted the wig. I fluffed the straight black bangs, but instead of flipping her signature braids in front of my shoulders, I wound them around and pinned them into place at the back of my head just as I had for Josie's party.

"I can," I said.

He sighed. "I had to try."

"And I love you for it," I said. I knew he only wanted me safe, but he also would never stop me from doing what I needed to do.

"See you in a few," he said.

We hung up and I put the finishing touches on my Wednesday look. I pulled out a few strands of hair, letting them fall in thin waves on either side of my face. My nails were still painted black, so I was all good there. I rimmed my eyes with heavier black eyeliner than I ever wore, and rimmed my lips with lip pencil, emphasizing the shape so I had the cupid's bow and full lower lip the actress, Jenna Ortega, had naturally. I took stock of the overall look in the mirror. Not bad, I thought. Not bad at all.

Juletta looked me up and down as I descended the stairs. I felt just like Wednesday probably did when she walked down the stairs at Nevermore Academy. That is to say, preoccupied with other more pressing matters. Namely, talking to the three most likely suspects.

None of that could happen until morning, though.

"That's a really good costume," Juletta said. "Really good. If you were a little girl—or adolescent, I guess, it'd be downright scary how right on it is."

I peered at her in pure Wednesday fashion. "Use the words 'little' and 'girl' to address me again and I can't guarantee your safety."

Juletta gawped before she placed the quote. "Oh my God, she says that to that really weird guy in the abandoned house, right?"

"Yup," I said, making myself smile, even though it was the

farthest thing from what I wanted to do. Without any evidence to actually arrest her, Orphie was still just someone of interest and safely back at home with Gavin by now. When I asked Gavin why he didn't share our theory with the other officers so they could investigate, too, he mumbled something unintelligible under his breath and then said, "Coming from me, it would just come off as a husband trying to direct suspicion away from his wife."

I'd always thought cops looked out for each other. The whole brotherhood thing, but it sounded like that wasn't the case in Bliss.

"What about Hoss? He wants the truth," I challenged.

"Yeah, I'm gonna talk to him."

I thought some of Deputy Shipley's motivation to keep the scrutiny on Orphie was probably her obvious crush on Gavin.

"Harlow."

And if the deputy was hellbent on proving Orphie was guilty, we had to be just as hellbent on proving her innocence. And that meant finding the actual guilty party.

"Harlow."

Which led me back to the three suspects.

Juletta cleared her throat. "Harlow!"

I blinked, refocusing on the here and now. She stood two feet away from me, waving her hands in the air to get my attention. "Sorry, what?"

"Geez. Where'd you go?"

I laughed it off. "Just lost in my thoughts. What were you saying?"

"I said, I'm leaving tomorrow."

"Oh," I said. She'd been entertaining herself so hadn't been around much. And honestly, her prickly nature aside, she wasn't a bad houseguest. "Well. Okay, then."

"Is there anything I can do while you're gone? Any sewing projects I can help with?" She rolled her eyes. "Kinda bored."

Was there? I was pretty caught up on everything at this point. My gaze strayed to the shelf in the atelier where three round tins—each probably forty or fifty years old—sat. Juletta followed the trail. "Buttons?" she asked.

I heard a sigh, so loud that I pressed my palms over my ears to block it. Loretta Mae was here. "Don't you dare," I muttered.

Juletta stepped back as if I'd smacked her. "Geez. Forget I asked—"

"No!" I shouted, entirely too loud. "I didn't mean you."

Juletta spun around, arms wide. "Who, then? We're alone, Harlow."

"I was just talking to myself. Truly." I hurried into the atelier and dragged one of my dress forms over to her. "I've been working on this," I said. "It's for Zinnia James, who's sort of my... my..." I was going to say benefactor because that's truly what she was, but instead, I said, "most high-profile client. She's the wife of Senator Jeb James. If you want to work on it a little bit..."

I trailed off as Juletta shrugged. The names meant nothing to her, but she walked around the dress form, taking in the vibrant brick-red silk and the pieces currently pinned together. Then she stepped back, arms folded, and studied it. "Not bad," she finally said.

It was a simple dress, which is what Mrs. James wanted. I'd made her beautiful lined suits, dresses, and even a gorgeous winter jacket in off-white raw silk with uneven black dots woven in. This dress was for the holiday party she'd be hosting so I had plenty of time, but if Juletta wanted to sew a few seams, I wasn't going to stop her. Better that then have her poking around the house, looking in the nooks and crannies.

I watched through the window and hurried out the

second I saw Will pull up in his truck. He barely had time to put it in Park before I hopped in. He grinned at me as I pulled the seatbelt over the black ruffles of my dress. "The kids are going to love your costume."

I smiled, sincerely this time. He was right. People at Josie's party had liked it, but Wednesday's target audience was more the high school crowd, so with them, I figured we'd hit a home run. Will was back in his Nevermore Academy clothes. "They'll love both of us," I said.

A short while later, Will parked in the high school lot. Weirdly, even though I was mid-thirties, it felt as if we were fifteen years younger and walking into the dance together. We hadn't done this as teenagers—since we hadn't known each other then—and a flutter of butterfly wings flapped in the pit of my stomach.

"You okay?" he asked.

"Yeah, fine." I dipped my chin the way Wednesday did. "Just getting into character."

We gave our names at the ticket table and waltzed right into the spookified gymnasium. A DJ was set up in the far right corner, refreshment tables lined the left wall, and teenagers roamed the open space in between. Just like at Josie's party, there were zombies galore, along with Ninja Turtles, a fortune teller, Sherlock Holmes, and at least three other Wednesday Addams. "Guess I'm not all *that* original, after all," I said.

Will took my hand and waggled his brows. "But you're definitely the best."

I spotted Gracie in her Dorothy dress and Holly and Libby in their Japanese anime cosplay outfits. They stood as part of a group, fully absorbed in their conversation.

Will and I circulated. "What's our job?" I asked.

He lifted one shoulder in a shrug. "I think we're supposed

to be on the lookout for, you know, alcohol, drugs, dirty dancing. That sort of thing."

"So I guess dirty dancing for us is out," I joked.

He waggled those brows of his enticingly. "For now anyway."

I swatted his arm, laughing. "What do we do if we see something?"

"Report it to one of the staff."

The turnout was good. The gym was full and I looked around, wondering if we'd even be able to identify any of the faculty. And that's when I saw her. Madison Blackstone.

Chapter Sixteen

Madison Blackstone stood next to two un-costumed middle-aged people who were either staff or parents. She was dressed in the same outfit she'd worn at Josie's Halloween party, reprising her role as Veronica Mars just as Will and I were with our *Wednesday* costumes. I threw my arm up and waved at her, far more energetically than Wednesday actually would, but I couldn't let a good opportunity pass. I hadn't forgotten her reaction when Jaclyn Padeski died. *I didn't really care for her*. Had that been just an offhanded comment or a confession?

Will shot me a side-eyed glance. "Let me guess, is that someone connected to Jaclyn's death?"

"Yes," I said with forced glee. "What luck."

"Yeah, what luck," he said, with a lot less enthusiasm than I had.

I grabbed his hand, pulling him forward. "Come on."

By the time we got to Madison, the other people she'd been with had drifted off. "Veronica Mars?" I asked with a knowing grin, noting the little buns on either side of her head like cat ears, the low-rise jeans and belt buckle, the t-shirt tucked in, and the camera slung over her shoulder.

"Very good. You really need to watch the show."

"It's on my list," I said.

"Will, this is Madison Blackstone. Madison, my fiancé, Will Flores."

Madison looked at the antique ring on my finger. It had belonged to Texana and Will had proposed with it at Christmas. "Congratulations. When's the wedding?"

"Soon," I said, glancing at Will. "Very soon."

Madison looked at Will. "You look so familiar."

"My daughter's in school here—"

Madison snapped her fingers. "Of course! Gracie Flores? She's your daughter?" He nodded and Madison continued, "Okay, okay! I see the resemblance. She's in the creative writing club. I'm the faculty advisor. Small world!"

"Sure is," Will said.

"She was at the party the other night. When that woman died."

"Was murdered," I said, watching Madison's reaction.

She froze for a long second. Blinked. "I'm sorry, what did you say?"

I wagged my finger between me and Will. "We heard they found a note that said if something happened to her, it was probably murder," I said, paraphrasing.

This time Madison's chin dropped. "Wow. Just...wow. And after all that talk about murder that day at Josie's. That's crazy."

"It's like she had a premonition."

Madison tilted her head, looking puzzled. "But why would she think someone would want to kill her?"

"You said yourself that you didn't really like her. You're probably not the only one."

She paled under the dim lighting of the auditorium. "I can't believe I said that. Such poor taste."

I couldn't disagree. "Like I said, I don't think you were the only one who thought that."

"What do you mean? I didn't like her—I mean, I hardly knew her—but so what? You don't go around killing people you don't like. And anyway, why would someone want to kill her? She was a hairdresser, right?"

"If we knew the answer to that, we might sleep a little better at night," I said grimly. I didn't think anyone was going to sneak into my house to smother me in my sleep, but if they did, I hoped Meemaw would summon up enough of a corporeal presence to pelt the culprit with every spool of thread, every pair of shears, and every other thing she could find to save my life.

Madison's brows lifted toward her hairline. "Do you think it's a...oh my God...that whoever killed Jaclyn is going to target someone else?"

"If she hadn't left that note, I might think so, but no. It seemed to be about her."

Madison was quiet for a beat, then she looked at Will. "Is Gracie okay? And Holly and Libby? They must be so shaken. You know, they can speak with the school counselor. Mrs. Talouse is really excellent. Very relatable."

"That's not a bad idea," Will said.

"They actually discovered the body," I added. "It was quite a shock for them both."

Madison's cheeks puffed out. She blew out the air in a loud stream, shaking her head. "I bet."

"Did you know her well?" I asked.

"Who, Jaclyn?"

"Yeah. I didn't know her at all, but it seemed like most of you did."

"I knew her, but not well," she said. "She'd called me,

though." She lowered the camera and looked at me and Will again. "Which was weird, actually."

I pasted a casually curious expression on my face trying hard to disguise the cauldron of excitement bubbling up inside me. I'd opened a door and Madison Blackstone had walked right in. "Oh? What about?"

"I don't know." The Monster Mash started playing and the teenagers were pulled to the center of the dance floor as if by magnets, turning it into a mosh pit. Madison raised the camera again, snapping pictures of them all. "She left a message asking me to give her a call."

I dipped my chin like Wednesday did, peering up through my lashes. "And did you? Call her back?"

Madison turned to me, smiling. "It's uncanny. You sound just like her."

"Like Jaclyn?" I asked, arching a brow.

"No, no. Like Wednesday Addams. All monotone and creepy."

I took that as a compliment.

As we talked, Madison scanned the room. She pointed her camera at a group of anime characters as she looked at the digital display. "Sorry," she said. "It's a hobby." She snapped a few more photos then took a step back and pointed the camera at me and Will. "Do you mind? Y'all have the best costumes."

Will put his arm around me, his expression dark and brooding. I stayed in character, pressing my lips together in pure Wednesday fashion. Madison snapped a few pictures, scrolled through them, and then adjusted the crossbody strap to swing the camera to her side. "So good."

"Can I get a copy of those?" I asked. She nodded and I fished one of my Buttons & Bows business cards from my small black drawstring bag, which also held my ID and my cellphone. I handed it over and she slid it into her back pocket just as I imagined Veronica Mars would have done.

"So sad about Jaclyn," I said, trying to bring the conversation back around to the murder. "I can't even imagine who could have killed her. And why? I mean, to murder someone? You have to have a lot of anger for that."

"Or fear," Madison said.

Now *that* was an interesting comment. "What do you mean?"

"I think anger would be more a crime of passion, right? But if it wasn't sudden, you know, in the moment, then it was —what's the word?"

"Premeditated?" Will supplied.

"Right! Anger feels more random. Or sudden. Unplanned, I guess. But fear, that could be more premeditated, right? Or am I just making that up?"

"Wait. So you think someone could have been afraid of something Jaclyn might do or say, and so they killed her to stop that from happening?" I asked, pretending that it was a completely new idea. "That's *so* interesting! Is that what you think happened?"

But Madison was only half listening again. She peered at a group of teens dressed as *Star Wars* characters. Han Solo, Princess Leia, Rey, and Kylo Ren. A few seconds later she sighed and turned back to us. "Gotta keep a close eye on some of these kids," she said. She kept one eye on the room of high schoolers even as she said, "Sorry, what were you saying?"

"No, *you* were saying that maybe someone was scared of Jaclyn and that's why she was killed."

She drew back like she'd been slapped. "No, no, no. You misunderstood. I'm not saying that's what *happened.* I'm just saying that *fear* might be a reason someone would kill another human being."

"Ah, so not about Jaclyn specifically," I said.

Madison gave a one-shoulder shrug. "Who knows? I've heard things."

I cocked my head in a very un-Wednesday manner. "Heard what?"

"You know, she was kind of nosy. Butting into other people's business. Lording stuff over them."

My head jutted forward like a turtle coming out of its shell. "Wow. Is that true? I didn't know that."

"I guess Josie didn't either since she invited her to the party. But I think it's one hundred percent true. One of the teacher's assistants here had a run-in with her. She wanted money, if you can believe it."

"Like blackmail?" I asked, trying to sound completely flabbergasted by the very idea.

"Exactly like blackmail."

As Madison turned her back to us and surveyed the room again, I looked at Will, brows raised in silent communication. So Jaclyn's proclivity toward holding people's secrets hostage wasn't a secret. "Did she pay? The teacher's assistant?"

"You know, I'm not sure. I try to stay out of other people's business."

As a general rule, that was a good practice. Unless you were trying to solve a murder, like I was, that is. "Do you think..." I pressed my palm to my mouth, careful not to smudge my lipliner. "Is that why she called you? Do you think she wanted to, I don't know, get some money out of you?" Because of a DUI, I finished in my head.

But Madison scoffed. "Good luck with that. First, I have nothing to hide. And second, I have no money. Teacher, remember?"

Hmph. A hugely underpaid essential job that people just didn't value enough. "Right. And really, what would she have thought you'd done? Jaywalking? Running a red light?" I laughed as I added, "Drunk driving? I mean, come on."

Madison turned to me, her mouth in a crooked line. "That's nothing to joke about," she said, any humor gone. "My sister ran a red light and hit another car. Luckily the other driver wasn't hurt, but it was scary." She pulled in her lower lip, biting down on it as if she could hold in the rest of the story.

"And she'd been drinking," I said, saying what Madison clearly didn't want to.

"It was her second time. She's in rehab now. Doing better, too."

"That's great. Good for her," I said as my mind processed this information. Had Jaclyn gotten her information wrong, thinking that it was Madison who'd gotten the DUIs? Or did she think Madison would pay to keep her sister's story out of the news? Either way, it sounded as if Jaclyn had never made contact with Madison. I pressed anyway, just in case. "Maybe she called about your sister."

Madison gave another half-hearted shrug. "I guess we'll never know," she said. She spotted another gaggle of teens all dressed in white sheets made to look like Greek togas. They were huddled together looking mighty suspicious. Madison went on alert. "Nice seeing you, both. Mr. Flores, I look forward to teaching your daughter," she said, and then she was off like a bullet train headed straight toward the Greek gods.

"Madison!" I called.

She turned around, distracted. "Hmm?"

"I was just wondering. Did you know Carrie Templeton?"

Madison hesitated. Glanced at the teens who had started to disperse. "Not personally," she said. I sensed there was more so I waited, hoping she'd continue. After another few seconds, her target gone, she came back toward us. "The woman my sister hit? It was her. It was Carrie Templeton."

I drew back, surprised. Whatever I'd expected, it hadn't been this. "Really?"

"Seems so tragic that she survived that car accident, only to drive off a cliff a few years later."

Tragic, indeed.

"Six degrees of separation," Will said after Madison wandered off again. "Only for Madison, it's just two degrees. From her to her sister to Carrie Templeton."

As we weaved through the crowd of costumed teenagers, I weighed everything Madison Blackstone had said against the idea that she'd somehow killed Jaclyn. She may have had the opportunity. She'd been at Josie's and Nate's party. She may have had the means, but we still didn't know exactly what had happened to Jaclyn, so that was the big question mark. And as far as motive, well, people only told you what they wanted you to know. Everything Madison had said was probably some form of the truth. The question was, could there be more to it? Like did Jaclyn actually speak with Madison in the same way she had cornered Orphie? Did Jaclyn actually try to blackmail her? Could Madison have killed Jaclyn to stop her from dragging her sister's dirty laundry into the public's eye? The bottom line was that I couldn't say with certainty that she'd played no part in Jaclyn's death and with this new information, her comment about not liking Jaclyn suddenly made more sense.

I was sure Jaclyn had been trying to communicate with someone in Josie's kitchen. It very well could have been Madison Blackstone. The weird connection to Carrie Templeton complicated the scenario even more.

I quickly texted Gavin and filled him in on my conversation with her. We can't cross her off the list, I wrote.

His response was a thumbs up.

Chapter Seventeen

We ran into Madelyn Brighton as we left the auditorium. "Hey-o!" she said. Without losing a beat, she lifted her camera and snapped a few photos of Will and me, glancing at the screen and quickly scrolling through the shots before she lowered her ever-present Cannon to her side, the strap angled across her body just as Madison Blackstone had hers. But for Madelyn, the camera was legit. It was her job.

"Oh my god, mate, you look brilliant. The both of you," she said in her cheery English accent, waving her hand around to encompass both of us. She was shorter than me so when she pulled me into an exuberant hug, her ample chest felt like beach balls against my ribcage.

She released me and stepped back, and suddenly her black hair looked electrified, as if an invisible magnet encircled her head, and the strands of her hair were steel, each being pulled out and away. In the time I'd known her, she never wore a wig, instead letting her natural hair shine. Oh boy, she was a sight for sore eyes. She was the one person outside of my family and Will—who was essentially family—and now Orphie and sort of Gavin...and Josie—who knew about Loretta Mae's presence at 2112 Mockingbird Lane. Her husband Bill was a professor at the University of North Texas, and she worked for the town of Bliss. She also freelanced, picking up photography gigs when she had the time. The first time we'd been alone together, she'd produced photos she'd taken which showed the rapid growth of flowers in my yard, as well as a swirl of white air hovering just above. That had been Loretta Mae in her earliest ghostly form.

Madelyn knew about the rumors, and then she'd seen the evidence. She had proof. At the beginning of our friendship, I'd been afraid of what she'd do with the knowledge she'd gained. But she and her husband were bonafide paranormal aficionados and I now knew she'd go to the grave with my secret—ironic since part of that secret was that Loretta Mae *hadn't* gone to the grave.

My charm had worked on her multiple times and had worked wonders. She tended toward the frumpy side of fashion but now she looked so put together and stylish. I couldn't help but smile with pride.

"What are you doing here?" she asked us.

Will put his arm around my shoulders and pulled me close. "I convinced Harlow to chaperon Gracie's dance."

"He promised me a date night." I cracked a grin and glanced back to the door of the auditorium. "And here we are. What are *you* doing here?"

"I'm an advisor for the photography club. I met with the kids and helped them with their camera settings since the room is pretty dark."

"And where's your other half?" Will asked.

"It's his bowling league night," she said with a smile. Her dark skin glowed and her cheeks turned pink, which happened whenever she talked about her husband or anything supernatural. "Now, fill me in. I heard about the poor woman who died at your friend's party. What happened?"

I looked around, wary of listening ears. "Let's talk outside."

"Better yet, why don't I come over to yours for a nightcap?"

She followed us in her car, pulling in behind us on the narrow driveway to the left of the house.

We went through the iron gate, over the flagstone path, and up the porch. At the moment, only Will and I were in costume, but on Halloween night, the street would be crawling with kids dressed as Ninja Turtles, characters from Star Wars and Harry Potter, including the triplets I was making the Luna Lovegood outfits for, and who knew what other creative things people would come up with. Seeing little kids dressed as kitty cats or lions or Raggedy Ann was half the fun of the haunting night.

The first thing I heard when we walked into the house was the steady hum of the sewing machine. Will and Madelyn trailed after me as I climbed the three steps to the atelier. Juletta sat at the sewing machine, her back to us. I stared at the dress form. The red dress for Zinnia James was finished and hung there looking simple, beautiful, and incredibly festive.

"Hey," I said as I moved closer to look at the details. The tips of my fingers danced over the bodice. She'd changed the design, reorganizing the pieces. Something about it felt familiar, but her nerve slightly—irrationally, since I'd given her permission to work on it—irked me.

"It's about time," Juletta said.

I spun around to look at her. "What?"

"You've been gone a good while."

I stared. It hadn't taken long for Juletta to pick up a touch of an accent. Something about her felt weirdly familiar, too, but in an inexplicable way. She looked different somehow. Her hair was mussed and she'd slipped on the old pair of cowboy boots I kept by the door. "You finished the dress," I said, turning back to it. I was about to chastise her for changing the design, but I stopped before the words came out, saying instead, "It's different than I'd planned, but it's beautiful."

Juletta left the sewing machine, her feet tangling under her. She moved like the Scarecrow from the *Wizard of Oz*, her legs rubbery as if she had forgotten how to walk. Had she gotten into some moonshine while we were gone? At my side, she cracked a smile. "I had to put my own spin on it."

I whipped my head around, this time to stare at her. She'd sounded even more Southern just then.

"Don't look so shocked, darlin'," she said. "You know there's always a tell. Always a way to know who made a garment.

The butterflies I'd felt in my gut earlier were back with a vengeance. *Darlin'*? Since when did Juletta call me darlin'? I stared. Looked at Will's puzzled face. At Madelyn, who seemed to know something was amiss, snapping pictures with her camera. I looked at the garment and noticed the zigzag stitch on a small section of the neck seam in the back. Not so much that anyone would notice—unless you were looking for it. I dragged in a ragged breath. No.

"I'm glad y'all are finally here. I was beginnin' to think you wouldn't ever get home."

I whipped my head around again, my mouth agape. A *definite* drawl had crept into Juletta's voice—more than just the faint hint of one—and those were definitely *not* her words coming out of her mouth.

"Cat got your tongue, Sweet Pea?"

As I inched forward, Earl Gray darted around my feet. I stumbled, but Will caught me by the arm, righting me.

"Darlin', you look like you're seeing a ghost," Juletta said, then she cracked a huge cockeyed grin. "'Course y'are."

Beside me, Will sucked in a sharp breath as I whispered, "Meemaw?"

"Whoa!" Madelyn moved to my other side, the camera still at her face, finger still moving up and down on the button as she kept snapping.

Juletta chuckled and her eyes sparkled. Only it wasn't Juletta. "I figured it out, Harlow Jane," she said. "And now I have somethin' to say to you."

I alternately froze and paced, froze and paced, my hands pressed against either side of my head, my fingernails clawing into my scalp. Finally, I pulled myself together and took Juletta's arm—because it still *was* Juletta's arm, even if it was Loretta Mae Cassidy's ghost force that had taken over Juletta's physical body. This was so much worse than her slipping into Orphie for a few seconds. How long had Meemaw been hanging out inside of Juletta, and what was happening to Juletta in the meantime? "Meemaw," I snapped. "You need to get out of there!"

Madelyn let out an awe-filled giggle. "Unreal," she murmured, then *snap, snap, snap.*

Meemaw was not known for listening to anyone but the beat of her own drum, but the split second I'd told her to get out, Juletta's body began to quiver, faintly at first, then growing and growing and growing until she was practically gyrating. A pang of anxiety shot through me as I registered what Meemaw had said before I'd ordered her out of Juletta's body. She had something to say to me. And oh how I wanted to talk to Meemaw again. To hear *everything* she had to say. I rushed forward, reaching for her hand. "Wait! I want to talk to you! What do you want to say to me?"

Juletta's mouth stretched wider than I thought possible,

and her face became elastic making her look eerily like Edvard Munch's The Scream. It contorted unnaturally and Juletta convulsed. "Haaaarrrrlllloooowwwww."

The haunting sound sent shivers up and down my spine like a live electric current zapping up and down a metal conduit. Orphie had been shaken when Meemaw had taken over her body. I had felt displaced. And shaken. And both of those instances had been for a fraction of the time she'd taken control of Juletta. Fear stabbed at me from the inside out. It was more important that Meemaw get out of Juletta's body than talk to me. "Stop!" I cried. "Leave her, Meemaw. Get out!"

Juletta shuddered, like someone had just walked on her grave. She jerked. Next to me, Madelyn's camera went *snap, snap, snap.* Will drew in another sharp breath. I stared, stunned, as Juletta heaved one more time. A burst of nearly— but not quite—translucent air formed into a vortex hurtled out of her body and for a moment, the room turned icy cold. I thought I could see the blurred features of Meemaw's face in the swirling funnel, but the air rippled and then popped. She was gone. The cold disappeared.

Juletta gagged. Coughed. Doubled over. Her knees buckled and she started to go down but Will sprung to catch her, gently guiding her back to the chair at the sewing table. "What the actual he—" she started, but the words died on her lips as she held her hands in front of her, flipping them over as if they might reveal what had happened.

There was no way I could tell her the truth. Far too many people already knew what Loretta Mae was—a ghost—and what she was trying to do—communicate by crowding into someone else's corporeal form. I didn't think I could trust Juletta with that delicate information.

Juletta gagged, dry heaving, then let her upper body fold

over until her head was between her knees. She dragged in quavering breath after quavering breath. I put my hand on her back, shooting a panicked look at Will. He shook his head and shrugged helplessly.

Madelyn had run into the kitchen, returning a second later with a small glass of water. She set it on the sewing table so it was there whenever Juletta was ready for it.

"Juletta," I said softly, rubbing her back. "Are you okay?"

I felt her shiver under my touch as if it was twenty degrees in here and the cold had seeped into her bones. My hand fell away as she slowly sat up. "I...I feel so...so s-sick." She turned her head, her skin pasty. When she spoke, her voice croaked. "Y-you're...b-back? Wh-what time is it? D-did I b-black out?"

I glanced at Will who already had his cell phone out. "Ten-thirty," he said.

Her face exploded in panic and she pressed the heel of her palm to her forehead. "Oh my god. Oh my god! It happened a-again."

I sat on the stool I kept at the table with the BabyLock serger, rolling it close to her. "What happened again?"

She picked up the glass Madelyn had brought and downed it all, clutching it, empty, in her hands. She looked up at me, her face even paler than it was a second ago—which I wouldn't have thought was possible—but there she was, as bloodless as a...a ghost. "I...that hasn't happened in...in a while."

"What hasn't happened?" I asked because I knew she wasn't talking about a ghost taking up residence in her body.

She inhaled again, deeply, then settled into steady breathing. "The dizzy spells. They used to get so bad. I...I passed out a few times, but usually, it's because I'm anxious. I talked to Orphie though and everything is good. I don't know...why would it happen again?" she cried as she put her elbows on her knees and cradled her head in her hands. "I thought I was better."

My heart dropped to my stomach, my own pool of anxiety forming there. I had to tell her the truth, didn't I? So she wouldn't think she was regressing. That she was at risk of panic attacks that came out of nowhere. But how could I?

I couldn't. I just couldn't. Instead, Madelyn and I helped Juletta up to her bed in the spare room. In seconds, she was out cold. Her entire being needed to recover from Meemaw's invasion. As we tiptoed back down the stairs, Madelyn practically buzzed from the excitement. "That was unreal, Harlow. Absolutely unreal."

She could say that again.

We spent the next fifteen minutes dissecting exactly how Meemaw was doing what she was doing and looking for any sign of her. "Loretta Mae?" Madelyn whispered. "Come out, come out wherever you are."

Will leaned against the wall, constantly scanning the room, keeping a vigilant eye out for her.

Nothing. "Maybe it wore her out, too," I said.

They both nodded. "Could be. She's definitely out of practice being, you know, *real*," Will said.

Well, that was most definitely true. With no sign of my great-grandmother, we moved on to Jaclyn Padeski. I filled Madelyn in on what we knew so far, including Madison and her sister's DUI.

"Maybe one of the others will know something," Madelyn said as she gathered up her camera. "I really have to run. I can't wait to see how these pictures turn out." I opened my mouth to say that she couldn't share them but she stopped me before I could utter a single sound. "Completely private, I know."

Bill was the leader of the North Texas Paranormal Society and Madelyn had been quick to tell me early on that the Cassidys were renowned in those circles. Despite that, I trusted her to keep her word. I just hoped she could keep a lid on her excitement so nobody in her circle of magic believers put two and two together to equal a real-life Cassidy ghost.

After Will left to pick up Gracie from the dance, I went upstairs. I startled myself when I looked in the mirror. For a while I'd forgotten I was dressed as Wednesday Addams. Honestly, though, it felt like I was living in one of the episodes of the show.

Chapter Eighteen

Juletta was still asleep when I left the next morning. Before I slipped out, I issued a warning to Meemaw. "You stay away from her."

The armoire doors opened, then banged shut, and I knew she'd heard me.

I had dressed like autumn with a pair of wide-legged plaid pants in taupe and green and burnt orange, an evergreen top, and a burnt orange jacket that tied it all together. The long-sleeved t-shirt wasn't a Harlow Cassidy design, but the pants and jacket were. I wrangled my dark wavy hair into a long braid in the back. For the time being, the tingling at the tuft of silvery hair that sprouted above my temple was quiet. Thank goodness for small favors.

First stop, Josie's. My one goal was to track down Abby Lassiter. "She works for CareHelp. She takes care of my grandmother. That's not an easy job. She's pretty cranky these days and she doesn't really talk." Tears welled in her eyes. She sniffed, then dragged the back of her hand across her face to whisk the tears away. "Abby's good with her, though."

I'd seen Abby in action with Yolanda Sandoval. She had a

nice manner. I'd also noticed how disconnected Mrs. Sandoval was. It's funny how old middle-aged people seem when you're really young. I remembered Yolanda Sandoval as ancient back when she was probably just in her mid-fifties. Now, in her eighties, she'd lost all the vitality she'd had. She hadn't uttered a single word when she'd been at Josie's house the day before the murder. I wondered how much she processed.

"I could never be a caregiver like that," Josie said. "It would break my heart."

I didn't think I could do it, either. I wouldn't be able to leave the job at home and turn off the emotions. As I drove Buttercup across town to a senior living complex, I fine-tuned the plan I'd come up with as an excuse for my visit, then I circled the parking lot until I found the building marked D. I found the elevator in the lobby, but opted for the stairwell instead, and eventually found the second-floor apartment.

Abby answered the door, staring at me in surprise.

I pressed my hand to my chest. "I'm Harlow? We met at Josie's?"

She wore her hair up in another high ponytail. She had her cowboy boots on again, but instead of wearing them under jeans, she rocked a floral dress that hit mid-knee. The first time I'd met her, she'd blinged it up like a good Texan woman. Today she elevated her outfit with a string of pale pink pearl-shaped beads. A lovely pendant sat at the base of her neck.

"Right!" she exclaimed. "Of course!" She looked over her shoulder and lowered her voice. "Are you here to see Mrs. Sandoval?"

"I am. I don't know if you know this, but I own a dress-making shop."

"Yeah, yeah. Buttons & Bows, right? Off the square?"

I nodded. "When I saw Josie's grandmother the other day, I just...I wanted to come see her."

"I didn't know you knew her that well," Abby said.

146

I smiled. "Josie and I go all the way back to elementary school." That wasn't actually an answer to her question, but hopefully, it was enough. When she didn't say anything, I kept going. "I feel like I have to make her something. I remember her always being so colorful, and now all that beige...Actually, I've been thinking of starting a community service project." I inched forward a bit, hoping she'd back up and invite me in. "It's for seniors and the infirm, like Mrs. Sandoval. If I can brighten someone's day..."

She lit up, like a lightbulb slowly coming on. "Like Make a Wish?"

"I guess. Kind of. And I thought since we both know Josie, and you take care of her grandmother...I thought I might be able to start here." I took another small step. This time she backed up and held the door open for me. The apartment was nice with neutral furnishings, a bookcase that spanned one wall, and a small eat-in kitchen. A very short hallway had a door to what I presumed was a bathroom, and another open to a bedroom. Mrs. Sandoval sat on the sofa, her shoulders hunched, her face slack. She looked...vacant.

"Mrs. Sandoval? This is Harlow..." She paused looking at me with raised brows.

"Cassidy," I provided.

She gave a single quick nod. "Harlow Cassidy. Josie's friend from school? She stopped by to see you, isn't that nice? She wants to make something for you."

Abby spoke in a bubbly manner as if she were speaking to a child.

Mrs. Sandoval tilted her head slightly, directing her rheumy eyes at me. She moved her mouth, but no sound came out.

"Yolanda?" Abby tried again. "Do you remember Harlow?"

Mrs. Sandoval just stared at me. "May I?" I asked Abby, gesturing to the chair next to the sofa.

"Sure. I'll get you something to drink." As she went into the kitchen, which was open to the living area, I made small talk with Mrs. Sandoval hoping she'd warm up to me, or that I could reach her. "Do you remember when you brought all the kids skull cookies?" I asked. I must have been ten or eleven. The school had done a *Dia de los Muertos* celebration and I could picture Josie trailing behind her mother and grandmother, whose arms were laden down with trays of cookies.

I watched Mrs. Sandoval closely to see if the memory sparked anything, but her face remained blank. I also waited for a vision—another burst of inspiration so I would know what to make for her. So far I hadn't gotten any inkling of anything, and once again, I worried about the state of my charm, but then I blinked and two things happened. I saw Mrs. Sandoval wearing a bright and happy yellow blouse with equally bright and happy orange pants. The colors against her dark skin were vibrant and brought pink to her cheeks. "I thought I could make you something," I said. "An outfit. Do you like yellow and orange?"

For a second she perked up. Her lips tried to curl upward and she gave the slightest nod.

A charge shot through me. I had made contact. "Okay!" I said, raring to go.

Abby came back with two glasses of water, mine without a straw, and Mrs. Sandoval's with one. "She nodded at me," I said, in case Abby hadn't seen.

"It's a good day, then," she said as she handed me my glass. She held onto Mrs. Sandoval's, guiding the straw to her lips and holding the glass steady while the old woman sipped. As she assisted her charge, so gently, another vision flashed in my mind. I saw her in a navy sheath. Very classic. So different from the jeans and cowboy boots she'd worn at Josie's, and from the dress she had on now. It was an outfit for a special event. I smiled to myself. My charm was in full swing!

After a few more minutes of small talk, where Mrs. Sandoval made small mewling sounds, Abby moved to her side again. "It's time for your nap, Mrs. Sandoval." She threaded her arm under the elderly woman's and helped her stand, then guided her toward the bedroom. "This'll take a few minutes. If you want to go..."

"I'd like to stay," I jumped in, even though a part of me just wanted to get back to my atelier to start sewing for Yolanda Sandoval. "I'd like to ask you more about her style."

"Sure," Abby said.

From the sofa, I heard the low pleasant murmur of Abby's singsong voice getting Mrs. Sandoval settled. While I waited, I scrolled through my phone. Without thinking, I typed Frederick Press and Bart Bolinary into the search bar. I gleaned a little more information. He'd had a heart attack and died en route to the hospital. Clogged arteries. It made me want to make some overnight oats and increase my fiber intake.

Abby came back into the living room. "She's settled." Although she whispered, I wondered if Mrs. Sandoval could hear us given the hearing aids I'd seen wrapped around her ears. She glanced toward the bedroom and frowned sadly. "She's getting worse. I don't think she has long."

"I better get to work then," I said. "I'm thinking of a yellow blouse and orange pants. Really bright and cheery. Does that sound like her?"

Abby brightened. "There's a few photos of her and her family on her dresser and she's got on a print dress in one and a bright pink top and jeans in another. I think she'd love a little color."

Perfect. "A blouse, or more of a t-shirt?"

Abby answered without thinking. "Definitely a blouse."

"I was thinking no collar," I said.

"And no tag. They can be annoying."

"And elastic-waisted pants, I think."

"Yep," Abby agreed.

I had stacks and stacks of fabric so I knew I could find something that would work for Mrs. Sandoval, but I asked one more question, just in case. "Can you think of anything else? A pattern she might like?"

"Mmm, not really," she said.

Well, okay. So I'd use something I already had. I started to stand with the intent of nonchalantly stopping at the door to ask her about Jaclyn, but I didn't have to because she brought it up.

"I still can't believe what happened at Josie's party. That lady? She seemed way too young to have something wrong with her heart or, like, have a stroke or something."

So she hadn't heard. My eyes pinched as I settled back into my chair. "The sheriff's department, they think she was murdered."

Abby recoiled, her mouth in an O. "Wait, what? Did you say m-murdered?"

I nodded. "It's so shocking, I know."

"Who would...kill her?" Her eyes filled and her face scrunched as she processed. "And why? Do they know why someone would do that? Oh my god, and how?"

All really excellent questions. "Did you know her?"

"I mean, no, but geez, murder?"

I shook my head to commiserate. "I know. And right in front of us at the party. Bold. I didn't know her, either, but it's so sad. And I heard she wrote a note. Like she thought it might happen." I said, planting the bomb and waiting to see if it would go off.

Abby's head jutted forward like a turtle. "What, like she knew someone was going to kill her? That's insane."

"I know. Completely insane. I don't think she named names, but yeah..."

Abby looked stunned. Shook her head. "God. Killed? I just...I can't even believe it. Small towns aren't what they used to be."

I had to chuckle to myself because Abby was too young to know what small towns used to be like. "Did you ever go to her salon?" I asked.

"No. I go to one over on the north side of town."

"Oh, right. I get mine done at Venice. The salon, not the city," I said with a laugh.

"I was going to say, that's a little far."

I started to rise again, putting my hands on the arms of the chair. As I stood, another question came to mind. Could Abby be the anonymous caller who'd put the target on Orphie's back? "You hung out with her at the party, didn't you? I thought I saw you dancing together."

Abby shrugged as she walked with me to the door. "I mean, we were all zombies, so why not?"

"Did you see her talking to a woman dressed as a flapper?"

She arched a brow and her forehead crinkled, just slightly, as she thought. "A zombie and a flapper? I don't think so."

I thought about the crossed out word next to Abby's name in Jaclyn's book. "Did you know Jaclyn had a little side hustle?"

We'd reached the door and she held it open. "What kind?"

"Seems she liked to blackmail people."

Jaclyn had spoken to Orphie. Maybe she'd come to my house that morning to talk to Juletta. She'd called Madison Blackstone. It seemed plausible she actually had tried to talk to Abby and Rowena, too. To plant the blackmail seed then step back to watch it bloom.

But Abby stared, openmouthed. "Blackmail?"

"Yeah. A lot of people. For DUIs and drugs and adultery

151

and theft, and geez, who knows what else?" Murder, I thought, but didn't say.

The color drained from her face like a clogged sink suddenly being freed of a blockage. "All those things? And drugs? Are you...sure?"

I touched her lightly on her shoulder, but she jerked away, spooked, cowering into herself.

"Hey, are you okay?" I asked.

She closed her eyes, her lids fluttering, like she was in REM sleep. "Sorry. I guess that just, um, triggered me."

Jaclyn's note next to Abby's name said *association*, which I still didn't understand. I adjusted my glasses, thinking, and a new theory bubbled up. What if Jaclyn had written Abby's name down so she could avenge her in the same way she'd done for Carrie Templeton?

That word: *Drugs*. *That* had triggered her.

Could Abby have been...oh my God...could she have been unwittingly drugged and then the...the unspeakable...? Could Jaclyn have learned who did it? I had to ask her. "Abby, did something happen to you?"

Slowly, she nodded and clutched her necklace so hard I thought she might break the chain. "In college. It was..." She stopped. Swallowed. "I was at a party. Someone gave me a drink and I thought it meant he liked me. So stupid," she said, angry with herself. "I woke up in a strange bed. My clothes. My wallet. My money." She sobbed. "My grandmother's necklace. All of it was g-gone." Her voice broke on the last part, then she gulped down her emotions. "I don't like to talk about it."

"I'm so sorry," I said. My heart ached for her. Her experience was every woman's nightmare.

As she finally released her grip on her pendant, I put two and two together. Her grandmother's necklace held meaning for her. I wondered if every necklace she wore since then was like a touchstone. She tucked a strand of hair behind her ear. Sniffed. Threw her shoulders back and pulled herself together. "It's, um, okay. I mean, it's not, but... Miles helped me get through it. I'm okay now."

I wanted to pull her in for a hug, but I knew I couldn't touch her. She might be okay, but she was still hurting. It was a testament to her strength that she could be so bubbly and empathetic given what she'd been through. I left, hoping I hadn't just opened a huge can of emotional worms for her that she'd never be able to stow away again.

Chapter Nineteen

Back at Buttons & Bows, I finished the Luna Lovegood costumes, packaged up the holiday dress for Zinnia James, and then dug through my fabric stashes. Eventually, I found what I needed, dug out two patterns for the garments, and I set to work making Mrs. Sandoval her clothes. I didn't know what any of her hopes and wishes might be—maybe to be aware again...*probably t*o be aware again. If that was it, then maybe I could help. I spent most of the day and finished the cheery sunflower yellow blouse. Now it was folded and wrapped in tissue, waiting to be delivered.

Before I started the pants for Mrs. Sandoval, I needed a break. And I wanted to speak to Rowena Adams. I loved a good mystery as much as the next person. I just didn't have a lot of spare time to read, and when I did, I tended toward *Threads Magazine, Where Women Work*, and other creative publications like that. I missed having a book going, though. What better reason to go to the library?

So far I hadn't gotten far in exonerating Orphie. I had a personal goal of proving Orphie's innocence to Deputy Shipley by handing over the real killer on a silver platter.

Rowena felt like my last hope. Talking to Madison and Abby did about as much for me as a sewing lesson from Bobby Flay might. Which is to say, a resolute nothing. Sure, Madison Blackwell had raised some red flags, but that's all they were. I'd added making an outfit for Mrs. Sandoval and maybe others in a similar situation to my plate, but I hadn't solved the main problem, i.e. why Jaclyn Padeski was killed and by whom.

The window for cool fall weather in North Texas was short. It might only last for a few weeks—if we were lucky. We generally went from a deathly hot summer to a chilly (and sometimes icy) winter, with very little fall or spring in between. When you got it, you had to take advantage of it, which is what I planned to do. I slipped on my orange jacket and strolled to the library, wishing I had a dog to walk instead of an ornery goat that kept me on my toes. I did have Earl Gray, but he wasn't much for being leashed up and trotting down the street.

The library was much farther from 2112 Mockingbird Lane than I realized. I hadn't actually stepped foot in it since I'd graduated from high school and left for college. Getting there was okay, but the realization that I'd have to trek back to the house when I was done, making it close to a ninety-minute roundtrip walk, kept looping in my head. I'd opted for adorable two-and-a-half-inch stacked heel lace-up rust-colored booties. They'd have been great as part of one of the Sanderson sister's outfits or on Miss Gulch from the Wizard of Oz, peddling away in the air on a bike with Toto in her basket, but for a long walk to the Bliss Library? Not the best decision.

Finally, I got there. The library was a modern-looking two-story building with a large sliding door leading to a foyer with announcement boards and flyers. Another door led into the library itself. Straight ahead was the circulation desk. It was enclosed by a plexiglass frame, guarding the librarian there from errant germs. To the right was a shelf of hardcover books for sale, all benefiting the Friends of the Library, and to the left was the children's section. Fiction, nonfiction, and the rest of the collection was in the back and upstairs. All in all, it was a nice library.

"Harlow?"

A voice from behind the plexiglass brought my attention front and center. Rowena sat on a tall stool behind the counter, a stack of books in front of her. She pointed the end of the gun-shaped device at the barcode on the book she was holding, checked the computer monitor, and then moved the book to a different stack.

"Hey, Rowena!" I said, plastering a big smile on my face despite my aching feet.

She laughed. "I almost didn't recognize you with your regular hair and clothes. I kinda like the Wednesday look." Her smile faded. "'Course I wouldn't wanna go back to that shit show of a night."

A man had walked up next to her as she spoke. His mouth pulled into a deep frown. "Rowena!" he scolded.

Rowena's heavily lined eyes bugged and she covered her mouth. "Oops. Sorry, Barry. It just slipped out."

Barry, whose name tag read Director, shot her a chastising look. "Hmm." It was all he said before shaking his head and walking away with the stack of catalogs he'd picked up.

Rowena rolled her eyes. "Okay, Big Brother," she muttered under her breath. "Anyway, do you need help finding a book?"

I did, actually. I'd always wanted to read THE ONE HUNDRED, not based on the cable TV show, but the one by Nina Garcia of *Project Runway* fame. It was a guide for stylish women everywhere. I gave Rowena the title and she promptly searched the system for it.

"Yep, we have one copy," she said. "Come on, I'll show you." She hopped off her stool and disappeared into the back room, reappearing on my side of the counter a second later. She waved her hand for me to follow her and led me up the wide staircase so fast that I didn't have a chance to slow her down and initiate any innocent conversation that might lead to plying her with questions that might provide answers about the murder.

Before I knew it, we passed another office smack in the center of the space and strode past rows of shelving, each end cap marked with the genre and displaying a few popular titles. She stopped abruptly in front of a section and quickly scanned the Dewey Decimal numbers attached to the lower part of the spines. In mere seconds, she put one finger on the top of a paperback book, its cover protected with a plastic coating, and pulled it right off the shelf.

THE ONE HUNDRED: A GUIDE TO THE PIECES EVERY STYLISH WOMAN MUST OWN

"This is it!" I said, flipping through the pages, instantly mesmerized by the stylized illustrations of women in fashionable clothing—even pajamas, each exemplifying one of the items Nina Garcia valued.

"Looks cool," Rowena said as she tucked the long black strands of her hair behind her multiple pierced ears.

"It does," I said, wholeheartedly agreeing. I had to hand it to Josie for having such a diversified friend group. It was eclectic, from Jaclyn the blackmailer, to Madison, a teacher, Abby, a healthcare worker, me, a dress designer, and Rowena, a goth-like librarian. Josie spread her friendship far and wide. Of course, *this* was the perfect way to start a conversation. "How do you know Josie?" I asked.

Rowena's darkly painted lips curved into a smile. "I run story time for kids on Tuesday mornings. She brings her baby in. Littles like Molly play with the board books while I read. It's a great way to expose them to language."

I couldn't help but arch my brows. "Wow, you—"

I broke off, slamming my mouth shut for trying to put Rowena in a box.

She smirked. "I don't look like the type to read kid's books?"

I circled my hand at her hair and ears and tattooed arms, then my hair and ears and tattoo-free arms. "Yeah, I guess," I finally said, knowing it was far too late to yank the pointy-toed boot out of my mouth for the guffaw. "I'm sorry—"

She waved away my apology. "Don't worry about it. I get that *all* the time, believe me. Usually, I give them the stink eye and say something like: *People are more than what they look like.* Believe me, that stops the judgment. Since I know you, I'll skip the stink eye."

"Well, thanks," I said, properly chagrinned. "I appreciate that." I liked the way Rowena Adams rolled. I redirected the conversation back to her comment downstairs when Barry had come up behind her. "That night was so horrible, though, wasn't it?"

"Holy sh—" She caught herself. "It sure was. That deputy who showed up? He came by to ask me if I'd seen anything strange. He's smokin' hot, isn't he?"

So Gavin had been here already. If he'd gotten any useful information, he hadn't shared it with me. I guess our collaboration only went so far. I ignored the smokin' hot comment. "Did you? See anything strange?" I asked. "Because I didn't. With everyone in costume, it was so hard to know who was doing what. Your Egyptian Queen was perfect, by the way. You rocked it."

"You rocked Wednesday, too."

We each smiled, acknowledging the traded compliments. "I still can't get over the fact that she died," I said.

"And not only that, but—" She paused. Looked around. Leaned closer to me and lowered her voice. "That deputy said she was murdered."

"It is shocking. And the crazy thing is that she thought it might happen! I hear she wrote a note."

"Wow. Really? What kind of note?"

Was it my imagination, or had her voice become a little shaky just then? "The kind that says if anything happens to her, suspect foul play."

Rowena's head snapped back like she'd been slapped. "Man, that is so dark."

That it was.

"I didn't think things like that happened in Bliss. I guess Bliss isn't the safe little town we all think it is."

Abby had said something similar. With all the death I'd seen since I'd moved back, I couldn't disagree. "It *has* had its share of bad stuff happen."

"Yeah, but murder? How? Did she, like, drown in the apple barrel? That deputy wouldn't spill any of the information and I've searched online. Zip. There's nothing about it."

"I don't think the authorities are saying anything about that yet," I said. Revealing too much might just put me back in the doghouse with Gavin and I kind of liked our current, friendlier relationship.

She pressed the heel of her hand to her forehead like she was warding off a headache. "It's actually scary."

She started walking toward the stairs again and I fell in step. "Sorry for upsetting you," I said, realizing that she might not be quite as tough as she presented herself to be.

Or was she a really good actress trying to cover up her guilty association with the crime?

She gripped the handrail as she descended, me one step behind her. "It's fine. It's just crazy that someone I sort of knew was alive one day and dead the next. And not just dead, but murdered."

I completely understood. Back at the circulation desk, I signed up for a new library card and checked out my Nina

Garcia book. I kept the conversation going as nonchalantly as I could. "Did she talk to you about anything?"

"Who, Jaclyn?"

I nodded. "I thought I heard her mention your name." Lie, lie, lie, but it was for a good cause. Maybe *she'd* been the anonymous caller.

"Only at Josie's that day."

"Not at the party? Or she didn't call you, maybe?"

Rowena's mouth pulled down into a deep frown. "What's going on? Why the twenty questions?"

I forced a smile and made up a story on the spot. "I ran into Madison Blackstone. She happened to mention that Jaclyn had called her for something, and my friend Orphie said the same thing. I guess I was just wondering what she was up to."

Rowena folded her arms like an added barrier behind the plexiglass wall. "Well, she never called me."

I couldn't get a clear pulse on Rowena. Was she irritated because she was actually guilty and here I was asking questions? Or did she think I was putting her back in that box? She looked dark, therefore she might be a murderer.

Either way, it was clear the conversation was done. I held the book up. "Thanks for this," I said. I gave Rowena a wan smile as I left, leaving her pale and distant behind her plexiglass barrier at the circulation desk as I started the forty-five-minute trek home.

Chapter Twenty

At home for the afternoon and the second half of my work session for Mrs. Sandoval's garments, I mulled. What was I missing? I'd replayed the events of the day at Josie's setting up for the party, and the party itself over and over and over. I replayed my conversations with Madison Blackwood, Abby Lassiter, and Rowena Adams, but so far, nothing had revealed itself. Only Madison's behavior had seemed slightly off, but even that was vague at best. She'd acted stunned, yes, but she'd also gone right back to snapping photos of and chaperoning the high schoolers dressed in their Halloween costumes.

Skull cookies and jack-o-lanterns and corn hole bobbed like apples in my mind, only I was searching for answers, not Granny Smiths.

I finished stitching the leg hems of the orange pants—so straightforward and easy given the elastic waistband—hoping I'd guessed her inseam measurements correctly. I'd thought about waiting so I could measure and know it was correct, but I wanted to get it done and take it over to her sooner rather than later. Abby had said she didn't think Yolanda Sandoval had much time left. That felt like a ticking clock. If I could have any part in bringing her a smidgeon of joy, I wanted to do that, and pronto.

I pressed the pants, then wrapped them in tissue and set them with the bright yellow blouse. I was antsy and despite the October date, my face was hot. I picked up a handwork project I was in the middle of, cracked open the top half of my Dutch door, and sat at the kitchen table. A brisk chill circulated through the farmhouse kitchen, cooling my flushed face. I thought best when I had a needle in my hand. At the moment, I worked my short needle, threaded with taupe-colored floss, up and down, pricking the tip through the fabric of my flour sack tea towel where I'd sketched an outline of Thelma Louise. The fabric was gripped taut in plastic embroidery rings. Stitch by stitch, the embroidered image of the Nubian goat appeared on the tea towel.

But no matter how much I tried to let the needle and thread clear my mind, it didn't work.

The cantankerous goat somehow sensed that I was thinking about her. The clomp clomp clomp of her hooves thumped on the back porch and a second later she nudged open the top half of the Dutch door that led from the porch to the kitchen.

She stood outside, her chin resting on the frame of the door's bottom half, the horizontal slits of her pupils taking me in, as well as everything else in the kitchen. She looked at me balefully and I met her gaze head-on. "Don't even think about it," I ground out.

She didn't blink. Didn't move a muscle. She stood there staring at me, those otherworldly eyes like lasers scanning every detail. Finally, I returned my attention to my embroidery, but a second later, she brayed, the earsplitting sound reverberating in my skull. I jumped in my seat, and nearly out of my skin. "Thelma Louise!" I hollered, slamming one palm to my chest. "What in tarnation are you doing?"

She moved her head, knocking her chin against the opening of the door as she emitted another raucous whinny.

I directed my gaze right at her but had no idea if she could even focus on just me. I chastised her with a firm, "You need to stop that, do you hear me?"

She bared her teeth just enough to communicate that I wasn't much of a threat to her.

Oh, game on. "You don't think I can make you stop?" I dared.

She let out another lusty bray. Challenge accepted.

Never breaking eye contact, I tossed down the embroidery hoop and grabbed the pencil I'd used to sketch the dastardly goat onto the flour sack, wielding it like a sword. For once in her life, Thelma Louise opted for the path of least resistance. She stepped back, her hindquarters bumping against the door, which was still ajar. She jumped at the contact, whipped around, and bolted out of the kitchen and to the back porch, taking the steps in a single gazelle-like leap.

"That's right, you best watch yourself, Thelma Louise!" I called after her.

A noise came from behind me. I spun around, pencil still at the ready, but an invisible force jerked my arm and the pencil went flying. It landed with a quiet bounce and then rolled. Instead of coming to a stop, it flew into the air again as if it had hit something that had propelled it upward. This time it landed on the table, and a split second later, a whoosh of air blew past and the pencil lifted into the air at an angle as if someone—a spirit, perhaps—was holding it, ready to write.

"Meemaw," I scolded, but the stern tone of my voice did nothing to stop her antics. She lowered the angle of the pencil and let the graphite tip rest against the seam of the tea towel, and then she started shading. "Meemaw!" I hollered as I lunged toward the table, snatching the pencil from her ghostly grip. "What are you doing? That's for Nana!"

I grabbed the handwork away from her invisible hands and waited for an answer I knew wasn't coming. Her only options were to flip the magazine pages, revealing words to convey a message, to steam up a window or mirror and write the message there—although I still had no idea how she managed to do either of those physical tasks—or to inhabit a body. At the moment only mine was available, and I wasn't about to welcome her in.

Only there *was* another body. As if on cue, Earl Grey sauntered by heading for the open door. I reached over to it, pushing it closed with the tips of my fingers, blocking his exit. The air swirled, a cyclone forming, but I held out my arm, palm facing it as I scooped Earl Grey into my arms. Meemaw was not going to get into his business. "He's off-limits, Meemaw, you hear me?"

The air fell still and all was silent. Crickets, in fact. Not a whisper of a sound or a distortion of the air broke the quiet. Meemaw had wafted off to some other part of the house. I set Earl Grey back on the ground and he skittered away. At the sink, I dampened a dishcloth and dabbed it against the pencil markings Meemaw had made on the tea towel. It wasn't wet enough to clean the area so I turned on the faucet, adjusting the stream of water until it was no more than a trickle. I put a touch of dish soap on my finger and rubbed it on the pencil, letting the droplets of water turn it into a light lather. The flour sack towel absorbed the water, which spread outward like a puddle. "No, no, no," I muttered as I shut off the faucet. I squeezed the corner of the tea towel, then flattened it out on the counter to dab up any excess liquid with a dry towel. The water on the nearly translucent fabric acted like an anecdote to invisible ink. Once the fabric was thoroughly wet, several large markings woven into the fibers were revealed. They were faint and seemed to be letters. It was like a reversed embossed manufacturer emblem, hidden away until the secret substance revealed its presence.

Someone pounded on the door, breaking the spell. "Harlow?" a woman called.

Ah...Orphie! I ran to the front room and yanked the door open. I grabbed her by the wrist and dragged her inside, throwing the door shut in one motion. A hand caught the side of it, stopping it from slamming closed. I jumped back, pulling Orphie with me. My mouth formed a surprised, "Oh!" then Gavin appeared, his mouth twisted into a frown. "Sorry, Gavin, I didn't see you!" I exclaimed.

I started to close the door again, but it stopped, hitting something solid. Will appeared. He smiled at me, bussing my cheek, the prickly whiskers of his goatee poking my skin.

"Tea?" I asked as they all traipsed after me into the kitchen.

"Sure," Will said, but the others didn't answer. When I turned, Gavin's frown was still firmly in place. Orphie's cheeks were pink from the cool evening and her eyes were clear. She looked better than she had the last time I'd seen her, so what was Gavin's frown about?

Will met my gaze, as baffled as I was. "What's going on?" I asked them.

Gavin held up one hand. And in that hand was Jaclyn Padeski's journal and ledger. "We're out of ideas," he said. "This is all we have. We're here to take another look."

Chapter Twenty-One

Before taking another step, Orphie spun around, searching the room. "Loretta Mae, you better steer clear of me, you hear?" she warned.

Will swallowed a laugh as Gavin stared at her, puzzled, but she didn't elaborate. Just gave him a sheepish smile. Orphie had said Gavin knew about Meemaw, but from his baffled expression, maybe he preferred *not* to believe. I couldn't blame him. Life was easier when you didn't believe in ghosts.

Meemaw had heard Orphie, though. The door to the wardrobe banged in acknowledgment. She'd heard Orphie. The question was, would she listen?

I set about making them each a mug of hot tea. Once that was done and we were all situated at the kitchen table, Gavin set Jaclyn's book in front of him. After fifteen minutes of flipping through the pages, nothing new had come to light. I fidgeted, drumming my fingers with nervous energy. Orphie put her elbows on the table and propped her chin on her fists. "There's got to be something. We're just not seeing it."

"Let's start at the beginning," Gavin said, scrolling through the notes he'd apparently written on his phone.

"Jaclyn was dressed as a zombie. So was a guy named Martin Moore, but his name isn't anywhere in Jaclyn's book. He has no connection to Jaclyn. The other zombie was Abby Lassiter. No known connection to Jaclyn, but her name *is* in Jaclyn's book."

The zombies had been on the dance floor together. Three zombies dancing. Drinking. Talking. Laughing.

Then Jaclyn's zombie body sprawled out on the porch, the apple barrel overturned, water spilling over the edge of the porch, and apples scattered about. I swung my attention to Gavin. "So she didn't drown, even though she was near the apple barrel."

"Definitely not drowned," he confirmed.

"Could she have aspirated? On her own vomit?" I asked.

But Gavin said no. "No evidence of that from the autopsy. That would have been a red flag. The bottom line is we just don't know. Sudden Death. It's a catchall for us not knowing and not being able to discover how the death happened. If toxicology reveals something, that'll help. For now, we have nothing to go on. She just stopped breathing."

We all processed this. Will broke the silence. "Are you *sure* she couldn't have been drugged?" Will said.

Gavin pursed his lips. "Nothing at this point indicates an overdose."

Will sighed. Scraped his fingers over his scalp.

I believed the ME's findings, but something about the idea of Jaclyn being drugged niggled in the back of my mind. What if...

"What are the possible ways she could suffocate?" I asked, then I continued, ticking the ways off on my fingers. "Drowning, but we know she didn't drown. Choking, but she didn't choke on her own vomit and they didn't find anything in her throat, right?"

"Right," Gavin said. "The ME said anaphylaxis is possible,

but there's no indication in her history that she was allergic to anything, and there were no obvious ordinary triggers in her system at this point. Also, no evidence she was asthmatic."

"And not a reaction to a drug she was taking?" I asked. "Or, I don't know, carbon monoxide poisoning?"

"She had ordinary prescription drugs in her bathroom. Nothing dangerous. And she was outside when she died so carbon monoxide poisoning is unlikely. She just...stopped breathing."

"Sudden Death," I muttered. For about the millionth time, I replayed the scene in my mind's eye. It was blurry like I was watching it from behind a layer of pea soup, but slowly, the mist cleared. We'd all gathered around Jaclyn. I felt a thready pulse, so faint I questioned whether it had been there at all. I started CPR. Someone had called 911. The paramedics arrived. "I was doing CPR on her," I said. I pressed my fingertips to my temples, trying to still my pulsing veins and the zapping at my hairline. Willing myself to think. To remember. "I was doing CPR," I repeated, "then the EMTs showed up. The first one—"

"Miles Fenton," Gavin said.

"Yep. He crouched next to me and...and...his hands. They hovered above mine. He said on the count of three, then he took over."

"It was seamless," Will said. "He didn't miss a beat."

"He found a pulse, but barely."

"And the other one?' Gavin had his cell phone in one hand, his thumb slid up the screen as he scrolled his notes. He looked up. "Ospry. Renee Ospry. What was she doing?"

I looked at Gavin. At Orphie. A sudden thought hit me. Had we missed someone with a motive? Could Renee Ospry have something to do with Jaclyn's death? "She's not in Jaclyn's book, is she?"

"Not unless she goes by a different name. And she wasn't

there. The EMTs came after. Focus, Harlow," Gavin said, the terseness he usually had when he uttered my name back full force. I sighed. I knew his congeniality couldn't last forever. "I want to hear it all again. What was she doing while Fenton took over CPR?"

"She was pushing us all back," Orphie volunteered. "Everyone was crowding around Jaclyn, and she—Ospry—was moving us back to give the other guy space."

I'd closed my eyes as she spoke, letting the scene play out in my mind. "Right. I kept thinking that any second Jaclyn was going to sputter and spit out water, or suck in air and her eyes would pop open. But obviously, that didn't happen. They pronounced her dead. That's when you showed up. And the rest you know. They put her on a gurney and wheeled her away."

My eyelids fluttered closed again, that feeling that I was missing something tugging at the cells of my brain. I came back to Will's question. Could Jaclyn have been drugged? Was there a drug that incapacitated?

Abby's story of being drugged in college hurtled into my mind, bouncing around saying *this, this, this.*

She'd been paralyzed by something put in her drink. Woke up not remembering a thing. Could the same type of drug have been used on Jaclyn, only things went sideways? Whoever did it gave her too much? Could it have been an overdose after all?

"Date rape," I said under my breath, then louder. Hoarsely. "Date rape. The date rape drug."

A hard line formed between Gavin's brows. "Rohypnol."

"Or ketamine," Will said.

"What about them?" Orphie asked.

Before I could answer, my thoughts scrambled in another direction. "On that one list in her book, Jaclyn wrote drugs.

169

That means somebody on her list of blackmail victims was involved with drugs somehow, right?"

"That could mean someone was dealing drugs, or taking drugs," Gavin said.

I turned. Paced the kitchen. "Right, but if she was black-mailing...or trying to blackmail someone who was doing either, they could have used those drugs on her." I spun to face them. "Couldn't they?"

"No toxicology yet, so it is possible," Gavin allowed.

I pressed my fingertips to my hairline to quiet the buzzing there. "If Jaclyn *was* drugged, how did it happen?"

The pictures sped forward in a blur until I remembered something. An electrical charge zapped me from the inside out. I grabbed Will's arm. "The cups."

"What cups?" he said, and then his face cleared. "Oh...the *cups.*"

"Through a drink!" Orphie exclaimed. "That's how it *always* happens at clubs. Someone takes a drink from someone else, not knowing they put something in it." The color had returned to her cheeks. She gasped. "You think Jaclyn was roofied? Or someone gave her Special K?"

Gavin looked skeptical. "Neither of those are fatal."

"They could be, though, couldn't they? If she took too much?"

"That's a risk," Gavin argued. "Both are sedatives. The dose would have to be really high to guarantee death, and even then, it seems iffy."

He had a good point. And who had the opportunity to give Jaclyn a drink laced with either of those drugs?

In my mind's eye, I saw Orphie at the punch table, a cup dangling from her hand. "You talked to Jaclyn at the party," I said, turning to her.

"Y-yes. She cornered me when I got there."

I grabbed her arm. "Where, Orphie? Where did she corner you?"

Orphie frowned. "On the porch."

"Oh." My face fell, but almost instantaneously, I reframed what I was thinking because of course, I didn't need to know when Orphie had talked to Jaclyn. What I really wanted to know was who had brought a drink to Jaclyn. A lot of people had drinks, but if we could place *one* of the three women—Rowena, Abby, or Madison—there with a cup that might have ended up in Jaclyn's hand... "I saw you talking with someone. By the punch table," I said.

After a beat, realization washed over Orphie's face. "Oh," she breathed out.

And then I remembered who I'd seen filling cups with punch. I remembered the zombies all dancing together, cups in their hands. Orphie and I spoke at the same time. "Abby."

Another image blasted into my mind. After we'd found Jaclyn...before the EMTs took her away, I'd seen Abby holding two cups on the porch, lifting one up as if she were offering it to her boyfriend. But he'd been across the porch and dealing with a dead body. The way he'd looked at her, pausing for a beat before shaking his head, refusing. She'd kept her gaze on him as she poured the liquid from one of the cups over the railing of the porch.

I thought about Abby's college story again. About where her name was in Jaclyn's book. I'd considered the idea that Jaclyn had put Abby's name in the wrong spot. That she'd wanted to seek justice for Abby, not blackmail her. But what if that wasn't the case? What if Jaclyn had put Abby's name just where she needed it to be? Abby, I thought again. She'd been at the punch table filling cups. She and the other zombies had been dancing with their plastic cups in hand.

"That day at Josie's house," I said, talking through my

theory aloud. "I still believe Jaclyn was trying to warn some-body that she knew something."

"You think it was Abby," Orphie said.

"I think so. When her boyfriend showed up, he'd asked what we'd been talking about. Abby had looked up at him and said, '*Death.*'"

I told them how we'd been talking about Carrie Temple-ton. How Abby had pointed at Jaclyn, telling Miles how Jaclyn thought the woman driving over the cliff and into the Pacific hadn't been an accident.

Before I could continue, the front door opened, the bell jingling. "Harlow? I'm back," Juletta called. She strode into the kitchen, gaping at us. Probably sensing the tension in the room. "What are you doing, planning a heist?"

Orphie rolled her eyes. "You're so glass half empty. We're not all criminals, you know."

Juletta's brows shot up, but she couldn't argue with that so she kept her mouth shut.

Glass half empty. *That* made me think. Jaclyn certainly saw the worst in people. She zeroed in on all the bad things they did, and then used that knowledge to her benefit. Some-thing else shot into my memory like a stray bullet from a shot fired two blocks away. "That day at Josie's, Jaclyn said some-thing about things not being what they seem."

When Juletta had first shown up on my doorstep, she'd been disheveled and had looked stressed. Since making amends with Orphie, she'd regained at least some of her confidence. I looked at her. "Do you remember her saying that?"

She nodded. "It was about seeing something, then later realizing that what you saw was not what you thought. Some-thing like that."

I clapped two staccato strikes. "Yes! That's it. We were talking about Carrie Templeton driving off the cliff, right? She said she thought the woman was murdered." The theory I was formulating felt spread out like tufts of clouds in the sky. I tried to gather them together into one mass. "What if the person she was trying to communicate to...to convey that she knew the truth...was Abby?"

"Like a veiled threat?" Juletta asked.

"Exactly."

Orphie slapped her hand over her mouth. "Wait, so you think Abby had something to do with that woman's death, too? What, that she drugged that woman before she went over the cliff?"

Her name was written just above Orphie's in Jaclyn's journal, which indicated these were the last two names she'd added with the intent to blackmail. If we assumed Jaclyn had been on the porch of Buttons & Bows and had overheard Orphie and Juletta talking about their so-called crimes, it made sense that Orphie's was the last name she'd written.

A few rows above hers...and above Abby's...the date was noted as mid-October. Another indication that whatever Jaclyn knew or suspected about Abby, she'd approached her about it recently. Possibly just after we'd all helped set up for Josie's party. "Jaclyn said she thought Carrie Templeton was murdered. She was very specific with that word. Murdered."

My head swam with hypotheticals. They pressed against my skull, building and building and building until it felt like a knob was going to jiggle loose and my head would explode like a pressure cooker releasing its steam. That blank line between Orphie's and Abby's names puzzled me. Whose name had she been holding it for? Someone who'd been at Josie's that day? Without any other clues, we had no way of knowing.

Chapter Twenty-Two

As Juletta left to go upstairs, I put the kettle on to heat up water. I took mugs from the cabinet and set a little basket filled with different types of teabags on the table. Once the water was hot, I poured, then brought Will, Orphie, and Gavin their mugs. When I went back for mine, my lips pursed just like Wednesday Addams. The flour sack tea towel I'd been working on caught my eye. That pencil smudge was still visible. I couldn't do anything more about it now, but I needed to keep my hands busy as we processed through our theories. I brought it with me to the table, and after I picked a chamomile teabag and put it in my mug to steep, I picked up where I'd left off, doing a running stitch in a pale gray floss along the outline of Thelma Louise's body. The cloth was still slightly damp where I'd rinsed it, but the hidden markings the water had revealed were hidden again.

I stared at the spot where I knew they were. Even if I couldn't see them, I knew they were still there. My gaze darted to Jaclyn's notebook. Something was there, but it was hidden away from us.

I dropped the embroidery onto my lap and picked up the

notebook, turning to the ledger in the back. To the names of the people Jaclyn had blackmailed. To the final list of names. Madison Blackstone. Abby Lassiter. Rowena Adams. Orphie Cates.

I stared at the page.

Orphie perched on the edge of her chair, watching me.

"What are you thinking?" Gavin asked.

"Harlow?"

What was I not seeing?

"Harlow."

Orphie's voice broke through the fog. My gaze snapped to the embroidery on my lap. To the damp edge where the markings had been woven into the fabric. To the open pages of Jaclyn's notebook. To the list of names. Madison. Abby. Rowena. Orphie. I ran my finger on the blank line above Orphie's name. Was I imagining it, or did it feel rougher than the rest of the page? I leaned closer. Peered at it. Tapped it with my finger as my head snapped up. "Something was written here then erased."

Gavin's head waggled in a jerky shake and his expression darkened from the idea that he'd missed something. "No, it's not."

"It was," I said. My skin pricked with the chill of a realization. I ran my finger over the line again, merely a ghost of the writing that had been, but I thought I felt faint groves under the pads of my fingertips. "She wrote another name here!"

"Someone else she was going to blackmail," Orphie said in a hoarse whisper, and then she shook her head. "What was *wrong* with her? Why mess with people's lives?"

There were a lot of people who did very bad deeds, and it was difficult to understand why. We'd probably never know what motivated Jaclyn. The pounding inside my brain was like a woodpecker slamming its beak over and over and over again. Whose name had she written here, and why? These names were in pencil. Everything else was in ink. Had she known she was going to erase it? Confront someone before committing to the blackmail?

"Everything else she wrote was in pen," Will said. "So why pencil for this? Because she knew she'd be erasing it? Was she trying to leverage her knowledge? Show someone she had dirt on them, and if they didn't comply, then she'd make it permanent?"

I stared at him. Blinked. That was *exactly* what I'd been thinking. We were in sync.

"So not someone already in the notebook," I said. Everyone we knew had been at the party and at Josie's the day before *was* in the notebook. So this name, whoever it belonged to, had *not* been there.

I jumped up and strode from the kitchen to the atelier and grabbed the magnifying glass I kept next to the sewing machine to help thread the eyes of very fine needles. A moment later, I shone the light of my cellphone onto the erased writing in the ledger and peered at it through the magnifying glass, enlarged and bulging.

I thought there was an I. Also an E, and maybe an O, but I couldn't be sure. It was just too faint.

From the corner of my eye, I saw one of the kitchen drawers open with a jerk. The next second, as if a tiny person sat inside and was launching things out, something flew across the room. My eyes tracked it as it arced, then landed with a single bounce followed by a roll.

Loretta Mae! I silently scolded my great-grandmother, shooting a glare with my eyes at every place I thought she might be.

Gavin gaped. "What the—"

He broke off when Orphie put her fingertips to his lips and shook her head. "I'll explain later, babe."

He stared, first at her, then at the pencil I'd used earlier on the tea towel that now lay still on the floor. "Explain what? How that just flew out of the drawer by itself?"

I shot a glance at Orphie. He might suspect but he didn't need to know for a fact that Meemaw was here. I raced through all the reasons why—the more people who knew, the greater the chance that the secret of the Cassidy charm would cease to be a secret. As it was, too many people knew about it. And what if the rumors spread and were revealed to be true? The Salem Witch Trials came to mind. And then there was the fact that normally Gavin didn't even like me! We'd broken new ground, but this might put the nail in that coffin.

But as I stared at the pencil, I instantly got over my agitation at Meemaw revealing herself, yet again, in mixed company —meaning those who knew about her (Will and Orphie) and those who didn't (Gavin). Because she was trying to tell me something.

"Oh!" I jumped up again, bending to snatch the pencil from the floor, then sat back down. I pulled Jaclyn's notebook in front of me

Gavin balked. "Harlow, what are you doing? That's evidence. If something's written there I can have forensics—"

I looked up at him through my lashes. "How long will that take, Gavin? As long as toxicology? Maybe Abby did this, but we don't know why, and maybe whoever's name was here will help answer that question."

He pressed his lips together but rolled his hand in the air so I went back to the task at hand. I turned the pencil to the side and with a very light touch, I shaded the blank space above Orphie's name.

When I was finished I folded the front and back of the notebook together, holding the loose pages with one hand and the page I'd shaded taut with the other as I studied it. The letters were faint. Scarcely visible. I closed my eyes as if to cleanse my vision, then opened them again, hoping to see a ghost of the letters revealed. Definitely the letters I and E and O but the rest was still unreadable. It seemed Jaclyn hadn't pressed hard enough to leave indented writing.

"It was a good idea, Meemaw," I muttered softly so Gavin wouldn't be able to hear, but it hadn't worked.

Chapter Twenty-Three

Gavin led Orphie out to the porch where the fresh air could perk her up. That left Meemaw, Will, and me to mull things over. Why would Abby drug Jaclyn? Was it because of Carrie Templeton? And if so, why would Abby have had anything to do with *her* death?

I knew that the name Jaclyn had written had to belong to someone she'd intended to blackmail. The fact that she'd erased it meant that something had changed. But what? I. E. O. I. E. O. I. E. O. Those letters meant nothing to—

And then it came to me. Oh no.

The weight of Will's hands was suddenly on my shoulders. "Harlow."

No, no, no.

His voice came at me again. "Harlow, what's wrong?"

My heart sank with the realization that the only person who had an I, E, and O and who'd also been at Josie's house that day was...Josie.

"It can't be her," Will said.

I blinked. I didn't want it to be, but *why* couldn't it be? I raised my brows with the question. And even if it wasn't actually her, would it be enough for Shipley to shift her focus from Orphie to Josie? Was I sacrificing one friend to save another?

"The letters aren't in the right order," Will said, instantly hauling me back from the edge of my doomsday thoughts. "If it was Josie, it'd be O, then I, then E."

I slapped my hand against my forehead and exhaled a sharp breath. He was right! "Oh, thank God," I heaved, and I let that fear go.

"Let's go through it again," Will said

We sat at the kitchen table sipping our now tepid tea. "Jaclyn collected stories at the salon. Carrie was a client. Nobody else was, though." What did we know about Carrie Templeton? "She was a nurse," I said, wondering if that meant anything.

I'd pushed aside the notebook, still open to the page I'd shaded in with the side of the pencil, but it suddenly slid toward me. I looked across the table to where I imagined Meemaw was sitting. The next second Will jerked his arm. He ran his other hand over it like he was brushing away a cobweb.

I sat up straight, my spine crackling. "Loretta Mae Cassidy, don't you dare."

Shock and the realization of what Meemaw might do registered on Will's face. He shoved back from the table, leaping up. He glared into the kitchen at large, no idea where Meemaw's invisible form lurked. "Loretta Mae," he said, sounding as if he were warning a mischievous child to stay away from a hot stove. "I forbid you—"

Before he could finish, the air in the kitchen suddenly whipped into a mini cyclone, upending two of the chairs, knocking things to the floor, and biting Earl Grey's backside. The little pig jumped and yelped, then scurried out of the kitchen.

"Meemaw!" I scolded as I stooped to pick up the note-book that had skittered across the floor. Just as I pinched my fingers to pick it up, it was swept away by another burst of air. As I reached for it again, it slid just out of reach. I was *not* in the mood for a game of cat and mouse. "Come on, Meemaw, knock it off."

I moved toward it again. The book flitted another foot, then fell still. I seized the moment and leaped at it, snatching it up before Meemaw could make it skip away again. I had no idea what this game was about and I had to stop myself from stomping my foot like an impetuous child. "Meemaw, what in the world!" I barked. "Now is *not* the time for your shenanigans."

Tinny faint laughter filled the room, growing and growing, the sound bouncing around as if it was coming from different locations. Will and I looked at each other. That was new. Meemaw had been able to clang the pipes and write with an invisible finger on my steamed-up bathroom mirror—and she was learning about using a host body—but this was the first time she, in her spectral state, had emitted that particularly haunting sound and tossed it around. She was getting stronger.

"Meemaw?" I said, my voice tentative for no particular reason. She was my great-grandmother, not some evil ghost, for goodness sake.

The laughter reverberated. Boomed so loud I was sure Juletta would come barreling down the stairs in alarm any second.

Will searched the room, baffled. Ran his hand over his face. "Loretta Mae, where are you?"

The room fell utterly silent, as if a switch had been flipped which turned off the spooky sounds.

"Meemaw?" I spun around, searching just as Will had. "Where'd you g—"

I stopped as a breeze rushed past me, ruffling my hair and the pages of the notebook clutched in my hand.

Will watched, wide-eyed, as the air curled around me, making me the eye of the cyclone, spinning me around, slowly at first and then faster and faster. "*Stoppp!*" I yelled. "*Meemawwww, stoppp!*"

Will shot his arm out grabbing ahold of my wrist, yanking me free from the swirling air. I stumbled right into his arms. Maybe *that* had been Meemaw's plan all along—land me in Will's embrace. She'd been responsible for us meeting in the first place, promising him sewing lessons for Gracie (courtesy of me) in exchange for some handyman work about the old farmhouse. Running into him—a stranger in the house I'd inherited—was our meet-cute.

This, however, was not the time for smooches and hugs. He stepped back, making sure I was stable on my two feet, then pointed at the notebook Meemaw had worked so hard to draw my attention to. "She wants you to look at that again."

The rubbing I'd done hadn't revealed anything. What was she seeing that I wasn't? And did her ghostly state give her super x-ray vision?

I sat at the table, pressing down on the crumpled page in question. Once more I studied it through the magnifying glass, then slid it all to Will. He did the same, finally shrugging his shoulders. "I don't see anything."

The chandelier above the table began swinging. There might as well have been a lightning storm raging outside from the way the lights began flickering. I stared at the fixture. It was definitely Meemaw making it swing, but why? "What, Meemaw? I don't understand!"

One side of Will's mouth quirked up. "Are the lights too bright for you, Loretta Mae?"

He lurched forward with an *oomph!* as a burst of air whooshed by behind him...or maybe through him.

I leaned toward him, grabbing his hand. "You okay?"

"Fine," he said, squeezing my hand back. He looked

around the room, once again searching for some sign of Meemaw's presence. "Guess she doesn't like my jokes."

"Guess she doesn't," I said, then to the kitchen at large said, "What are you doing, Meemaw?" If anyone had been walking by, looking in the window, I'd have looked ridiculous talking to the empty space of the room, but I didn't care. "You're makin' me crazy!"

The lights flickered again. Frenetically. That was the only word that described the manic energy pulsing and shooting through the bulbs. Another breeze blew, riffling the paper in the notebook until Will slammed his hand down on it. What did she think the paper could tell me?

I jumped when the back door burst open. Nana waltzed in, kicking off her Crocs, which revealed her pristine white socks. It was as if they were brand new, straight from the package, but I knew that wasn't the case. Nana's goat-whispering wasn't her only charm. She also had the curious—and pointless—ability to keep her socks whiter than white.

She looked at me. At Will. At the swaying light fixture. "Howdy do, Mama," she said to her ghostly mother.

As Thelma Louise poked her head through the door, craning her neck to look around Nana, the lights flickered and winked in response. The goat let out a spooked bray as her sideways eyes took in the entire kitchen. I peered at her. At the chandelier. Scanned the room for any other physical sign of Meemaw.

"Meemaw?" I asked. "Come on. What are you trying to tell me?"

The lights continued to wink and Thelma Louise let out another cry. She scurried back, turned, and leaped off the porch. I couldn't help but smile. I had ammunition now whenever that dastardly goat tried to get *my* goat. I could just summon Meemaw...if only Meemaw *came* when summoned.

"What's she doin'?" Nana asked, talking about Meemaw, not the queen of her herd.

"Flashing the lights, but we don't know why," Will said.

Nana folded her arms over her chest. "What's that you're holdin'?" she asked.

I held the paper up and explained what I'd tried to do by shading the area where I thought indented writing might reveal something. I followed Nana's gaze as she looked up at the chandelier, then down at the paper in my hand. It hit me like a kick to the gut by a horse's hoof. The light. Meemaw wanted me to hold the paper up to the light.

Dumb, dumb, dumb. How could I have not thought to do that? And why had it taken me so long to realize that *this* was what Meemaw was trying to get me to do? Will went to the light switch on the wall and turned the knob, making the bulbs illuminate at full brightness. He nodded at me and I lifted the journal, holding the page to the light, letting it shine through. I saw the faint I, E and O again, but nothing else.

"Wait," I said, and I hurried to the kitchen drawer that held pens, a book of stamps I'd had for a year and a half—letter-writing was a dying art so the stamps would last me another eighteen months, probably—matches, a lighter, a collection of miscellaneous batteries, and the thing I was looking for: a flashlight that was stronger than the one on my cellphone. I grabbed it and two seconds later I held it under the paper, Will by my side. The I and the E and the O were a little more visible with the direct light shining under them, but a moment later other letters started to materialize, so faint I had to squint, but under the brightness of the flashlight's beam, they were definitely there. Letters that took my breath away.

Will stared. "Wait, is that the—"

I looked at him. Felt the blood drain from my face. Nodded. *This* was the other person Jaclyn had thought to blackmail? My brows pinched together because the name didn't make sense.

At that moment, Gavin strode back into the kitchen, his hand on Orphie's lower back, guiding her protectively. He looked at me and as he registered my wide eyes, my mouth in an O, he surged forward. "What's going on?" he asked me, followed with a quick—and dare I say it—concerned, "Are you okay?"

I opened my mouth to speak, but the words wouldn't come out. Gavin notched his thumb in my direction, speaking to Will. "Is she okay?"

Will's lips pressed together. He shook his head as he took hold of the notebook, still open to the page with the pencil shading, and flashlight I held, gently prying them from my hands. Somberly, he handed them both to Gavin. Gavin did what I'd done, flicking the switch of the flashlight and holding the beam directly under the paper, aimed right at the shaded section. "Holy sh—," he muttered under his breath.

My thought exactly.

Chapter Twenty-Four

Miles Fenton.

He had been at Josie's house the day before but he hadn't been at Josie's part—.

But then I gasped because he *had* been there the night Jaclyn died. Of course he had.

"He's a paramedic. So how would he have known Jaclyn?" Will asked, and then more slowly, "Wait. He's a paramedic. Didn't you say the woman who died—Carrie Templeton —she—?"

I nodded, and then as if he'd volleyed his thought straight into my mind, the answer came to me with a whoosh. "A nurse. At the ER." And then more slowly. "Where their paths would have crossed."

"They must have," Gavin said.

The gears in my brain turned, slotting into place bit by bit. "What if Carrie Templeton knew something about him...or suspected him of something and—

"He killed her to keep her quiet?" Orphie offered. "Whatever she knew about him had to be bad."

Gavin was already on the phone. I thought he'd called the

station, but the second he spoke, I knew it was to his daddy. He gave him Fenton's full name and filled him in. The second he hung up, he turned to me again. "But would he have reason to kill Jaclyn Padeski?"

"Yes," I said, fully confident the answer was right. "Because Carrie sat in Jaclyn's salon chair and told her whatever it was she suspected. Maybe Jaclyn was going to blackmail him, or maybe not, but then Carrie *died*. That may have changed everything. She wrote his name down with plans to blackmail him for that. For murder."

"But she erased his name? Why would she change her mind?" Orphie asked. "And why is Abby's name still there?"

Orphie posed the hypothetical and we all looked toward the ceiling, thinking. "Maybe Miles paid quickly. She may have erased his name but just never got around to updating her notes?"

I went back to Abby's name. The word in the column next to it said: Association, but crossed out. I pondered that, still unable to figure out what it meant. I ran through all the local associations I could think of. There was the Women's Health Coalition. There were associations for veterans and garden clubs and even paranormal societies like the one Madelyn Brighton was part of. Figuring out what kind of association Jaclyn had been referring to felt like finding an embroidery needle in a haystack.

Abby and Miles. Miles and Abby. Miles's name, then Abby's. Association. Association. Association. I repeated the word over and over in my head, then thought of phrases. Football association. FIFA. Parent-Teacher associations. Free association. In association with. Guilt by association. National Rifle Association. In association with—

My brain screeched to a halt. "Guilt by association," I murmured, then louder, "Guilt by association."

They all turned to look at me. "In the notebook, Jaclyn

wrote *association* next to Abby's name. Could she have meant *guilt* by association?"

"But she crossed it out," Orphie reminded me.

Right. Why would she do that? Why cross it out? I posed another *What if.* What if Jaclyn *thought* Abby was guilty by association to Miles, but changed her mind."

Will threw out a counterargument. "If that's the case, why not erase her name altogether, like she erased Miles Fenton's?"

I saw Abby ladling punch into cups. Handing one to Jaclyn. Later pouring out whatever remained. Nesting those two cups together. "Because she *was* guilty."

"Did she write something next to Fenton's name? And then erase it?" Will asked.

That was a good question. I'd only shaded where I thought the name was written. I ran my finger over the spot next to where I'd already shaded. Bent to study it. It *did* look like something had been written there and then had been erased. I picked up my pencil, lightly shading the area. Just like the single letters I, E, and O, which had revealed themselves the first time I'd done this, then shone the flashlight beam under the paper. Two more very faint letters materialized. C and T. "Carrie Templeton," I said, holding the notebook out so they could see the indented writing, still barely noticeable.

"So she suspected foul play in Carrie Templeton's death based on what Carrie had suspected, but she placed the blame on Abby, not on Miles," Gavin said.

Orphie rubbed her temples. "I'm confused. Do you think Abby killed Jaclyn then? Because she was already dead...or pretty much dead by the time he got there."

"Remember, though, Rohypnol and ketamine aren't fatal," Will reminded me, "assuming that's what Abby gave her. Unless she gave her so much that it definitely would kill her."

"Wait," I said. My voice lowered as another idea surfaced. "What if the drug was never *supposed* to kill her?"

They all stared at me, waiting. A chill wound through me, curling around my spine. "Who drove the ambulance?"

Gavin considered my question. He tilted his head. Blinked. Then his spine stiffened. He seemed to know what I was getting at. He grabbed his phone and started texting someone. Not a second later, he looked me dead in the eyes. "Ospry drove. Fenton was in the back with the body."

I felt my body go cold. "What if it wasn't a *body* at that point, but still a *patient*?"

Will ran his hand down his face and gave a low whistle. "Wow."

"Yeah," Gavin said.

"Wait, wait, wait." Orphie scrunched her eyes. Put her elbows on the table. Propped her chin on her fists. She looked up at Gavin, the color drained from her face and her eyes welled. "What are you saying? That Jaclyn was *alive* when she was in the ambulance? But they said she was dead! They gave a time of death!"

I'd learned long ago that people saw what they wanted to see. They saw what they *expected* to see. In this case, we were *told* Jaclyn was dead by one of the people who had come to save her. Why wouldn't we believe Miles Fenton, the EMT? I let out a shaky breath. "They must have been in it together. Abby drugged her and Miles finished it in the ambulance." I shuddered, trying not to picture Miles holding something over Jaclyn's nose and mouth, stopping the flow of oxygen completely. I turned to look at Gavin. "That would explain the Sudden Death, right? There was no clear sign of overdoes. Whatever drug sedated her could probably be blamed for her death. If it was Rohypnol, who would suspect that a woman gave it to her? Abby would never even be suspected. If Jaclyn was declared dead at the scene, then it would be called a freak accident."

It was bold and callous and very, very premeditated.

Something else niggled in the back of my mind. Whatever it was, I couldn't quite shake it free. I wished I had a wand like Professor Dumbledore's and could hold it to my temple, pulling out isolated thoughts. I spotted my laptop where I'd left it after searching Bart Bolinary and children's authors in Bliss. I'd done Internet searches of Carrie Templeton's name multiple times. Now I grabbed the computer and Googled her name one more time. Skimmed the first article. Then the second. I kept scrolling and scrolling, looking for something I'd missed. Some clue as to what Carrie suspected Miles Fenton of. Nothing in any of the initial articles jumped out at me so I went back to the search results. On the second page, Carrie's name was highlighted as a keyword in the obituary of a woman named Maxine Watson. I clicked and skimmed. Maxine Watson was Carrie Templeton's aunt. She had a relapse of breast cancer, which sadly took her life. She died at home surrounded by friends and family, including her children and her niece. A photo of Maxine Watson as a young woman was next to the article. She was lovely and the photo was reminiscent of the 1960s with the sleeveless white dress and the pillbox hat. She had on a pearl necklace with a large pendant in the middle. I gasped. Enlarged the article, readjusting it on the screen to get a better look at the photo. At the pendant. Because I recognized it. I'd seen it. My blood ran cold in my veins. On Abby Lassiter.

"That necklace!" I said, hearing the screech of my voice in my head. I told them I'd seen that pendant on Abby, but I knew we needed proof. I opened a new tab to type in the health care company Abby worked for but my mind went blank. *Think!* Josie had told me. HomeHealth? HealthCare?

No, no, no. Those weren't right. Oh! Not *health*, but *help*. HomeHelp...no. Then it came to me. CareHelp. While the others watched, I searched. Found the number. Grabbed my phone and dialed, putting the call on Speaker. A woman answered on the second ring. As soon as she'd completed her greeting, I launched into my question, ad-libbing as I talked, forcing myself to speak slowly. Calmly. "My friend hired someone from CareHelp a while back for her aunt. Maxine Watson? I think the woman might be a good fit for my mom..."

I left the sentence hanging there in hopes the woman on the other end of the line would pick up and carry on. "Of course, I remember Maxine Watson. Let's see, yes, I believe it was Abigail who cared for her."

Bingo! "Aw, that's great. Thank you! I appreciate the help."

"Wait!" The woman's command stopped me from hanging up. "Would you like to make an appointment? To talk about care for your mother?"

I did a mental head slap for forgetting to bring my story full circle. "I do!" *Not,* I thought. Thankfully Nana and Mama were nowhere near needing such care. "I just need to look at my schedule," I said. "I'll call back!"

"Wonderful. I look forward to talking with you about how CareHelp can support—"

I hung up before she could finish and looked up to find Will and Gavin and Orphie staring at me.

"Abby Lassiter was the caregiver for Carrie Templeton's aunt," Gavin said. "Unbelievable."

"And..." I pulled up Maxine Watson's obituary again, zoomed in on the photograph, and held it out to show them. "Abby was wearing *that* pendant when I saw her the other day." I tapped the screen for emphasis. "*That pendant.*"

Jaclyn had said things aren't always what they seem. Rowena had said something similar. Abby was a caregiver, but was that all? "Could it have been a gift?" Orphie asked, but I could hear the skepticism in her voice.

"It's possible," I said. "What if Abby stole it?"

"What if that's what Carrie Templeton suspected? That her aunt's caregiver was a thief?" Will shook his head. "Not worth killing over."

A shiver passed through me again, chilling me from the inside out. "Unless…"

Orphie exhaled a distraught breath. "Unless what?"

"Unless she sped up Maxine Watson's death," I said.

And then I remembered something. "What's Madison Blackstone's phone number?" I asked Gavin.

I could see his wheels turning. See him about to drill me, but then he flipped through his little pad and rattled it off. I dialed. It rang and rang and rang. With each unanswered second that passed, a vice tightened around my heart. At the last second, just before I was sure it was going to click over to voicemail, she answered with a breathless, "Hello!"

Quickly, I put the call on Speaker and told Madison what my question was. "He's right across the hall." She hesitated. "Do you want me to get him?"

I stopped myself from shouting. "Yes," I said, drumming my fingers on the table.

Will, Gavin, and Orphie watched me. "What are you—" Will started, but broke off when a man's voice said, "Hello?"

"Hi. Mr. Templeton. You don't know me and I'm so sorry to bother you. I'm sorry for your loss."

"Okay. Well, thanks," he said, sounding baffled. "What's this about?"

"My name is Harlow Cassidy. I just have a quick question for you. I know it's out of the blue, but it's about your great-aunt."

"Maxine?" he asked, his voice rising in surprise. "What about her?"

"She had a caregiver."

"That's right."

"Sir, what's her name?"

"Abby Lassiter."

Ding ding ding! More confirmation of what I'd thought. "Right. Yes. I'm just wondering if you...did you ever have any...*trouble* with her?"

He hesitated before saying, "What kind of trouble?"

"I don't know. I guess I'm wondering if...after your aunt passed, were any of her things missing?"

I heard his sharp inhale. "Why?" he blurted, then more calmly, "What do you know?"

"I don't know anything for sure," I said. "It's just, that I saw a photo of your aunt in the paper. Her obituary. She was wearing a beautiful strand of pearls and there was a pendant. And I was just wondering—"

"Goddammit," he said, cutting me off. "My mother was right. She said that girl stole it and that she—"

I heard voices in the background and John Templeton's muffled voice as if he had pressed the phone to his chest. After a few seconds, he came back. "Maddie said this is about the woman who just died. Jaclyn something?" Another murmur. "Right. Padeski," he said.

I glanced at Gavin. He had his pad of paper out and was scribbling notes. He nodded at me to keep going, so I answered truthfully. "It is."

"That pendant was missing when Aunt Maxine passed, which didn't make sense. My aunt told my mother it was for her. That she wanted her to have it. My mother, she looked everywhere for it. She complained to the company that girl worked for, but they said this sort of thing happens all the time. That people whose faculties have deteriorated misplace things, or give them away."

"Was anything else missing?" I asked.

He heaved a sigh. "Oh yeah. Quite a few things. Abby said Maxine gave stuff away all the time, to random people when she took her for walks in her wheelchair. Pretty hard to disprove that when she's claiming Maxine gave it to strangers."

It sure was.

"My mom was *sure* it was all stolen. She shouldn't have died, you know," he said.

"It was a terrible accident," I agreed.

"Not my mom, but yes, it was. Terrible. She was a careful driver, so it still doesn't make sense. And there is no way she did it on purpose."

I looked at Gavin, but he shook his head. He had read my mind and was telling me not to say a word about Carrie Templeton's death and our suspicions. That thought left my head the next second when John continued with, "I'm talking about Maxine. My mom always said she shouldn't have died. Not then. Not yet."

I pushed up my glasses to the top of my head and pinched the bridge of my nose. "What do you mean?"

"I mean she was doing well. In remission. The caregiver was just to give my mom a break, but then Aunt Maxine started declining. My mom needed more help with her. A month later she was dead. They tried to resuscitate her on the way to the hospital, but she just...died. They should have saved her. The doctors said she had more time."

After I hung up with John Templeton, I sat there frozen. Maxine Watson had died en route to the hospital. So Carrie Templeton really *had* suspected foul play in her aunt's death. And the scenario was eerily similar to what had happened to Jaclyn.

"It's something to work with," Gavin said. He grabbed Orphie's hand, pulling her up. "Let's go, baby."

I stared. "Where are you going?"

"All of this is circumstantial. Now I need to find some evidence." They started toward the door, but he stopped and turned back. "Good job, Harlow," he said, and then they were gone.

Chapter Twenty-Five

Will and I stood side by side at the front door, him rocking back on the heels of his boots and me absently fingering the tissue paper wrapped around the blouse and pants I'd made for Yolanda Sandoval, which sat on the little entry table.

The tissue crinkled under my touch. "I wish we could *do* something."

"Gavin is on it," he said.

I knew he was, but I felt useless. Surely there was something we could do in the mean time.

I worried the tissue between my fingertips, rubbing and rubbing and rubbing. And then it tore. I grumbled and frowned at the gaping split that revealed the sunflower yellow blouse inside. I muttered a frustrated, "Oh."

And then I blinked. Stared at the torn tissue and the blouse. Everything came to a screeching halt. I'd seen Abby wearing that pendant when I'd gone to Yolanda Sandoval's. Yolanda Sandoval, who was Josie's grandmother. And who had become worse and worse and worse while under Abby's care. "Oh no."

Will stood back, arms folded like a barrier over his chest. "What's wrong?"

"Josie's grandmother is...she's...Abby's her caregiver. When I saw her, she was really out of it and Josie and Abby both said she's been declining." Good days and bad days, Abby had said. My insides turned upside down, my heart beating like the flapping wings of a thousand bats. "What if..." I couldn't even bear to say it, but I had to. The words came out in a panic. "What if Abby's planning to do the same thing to Mrs. Sandoval?"

Two seconds later, I grabbed the orange pants and the yellow blouse in their wrapped and torn tissue and shoved them into one of the Buttons & Bows gift bags. I snatched my keys and purse. "Come on!" I hollered, already out the door and halfway down the porch steps.

Will thundered down the steps behind me. "Come on to where?"

"Mrs. Sandoval's!" I said as I threw myself into the driver's seat of Buttercup, buckled up, and jammed the key into the ignition. It sputtered to life as Will slammed the passenger door closed. He turned to look at me, but I threw the truck into reverse and jolted backward out of the driveway. Will grabbed the seatbelt and strapped himself in. He didn't bother to try to convince me we shouldn't charge into an old lady's apartment with a possible—suspected—probable murderer there. He knew me too well by now. Instead, he tugged his phone from his pocket. Less than a minute later, Buttercup was lumbering down Mockingbird Lane toward the north side of town and Will was leaving a message for Gavin, telling him where we were going...and why.

He held the phone in his hand, looking at it expectantly like he was willing Gavin to call him back. "We can't just barge in there and accuse this girl of murder, Harlow."

Whenever Will called me Harlow instead of Cassidy, I

knew he was serious. I glanced at him. "I know. But I have the outfit I made for Mrs. Sandoval. We can go in to give it to her and make sure she's safe until Gavin gets there with his evidence."

He nodded, but he didn't look happy about it. His goatee and olive skin and smoldering eyes were pinched and troubled, making it clear he didn't particularly like this plan. He'd rather wait for Gavin, but I couldn't do that. *We* couldn't do that. I pushed my foot down on the gas, urging Buttercup to go faster. We barreled along until finally, we reached the senior living complex I'd visited just a few days before. It felt as if nothing at all had happened to solve the murder of Jaclyn Padeski between then and now…and at the same time, it felt like everything had happened and now everything was on the line. I didn't know if it was imminent, but I didn't want Mrs. Sandoval to die before she was good and ready. I parked at a crazy angle, grabbed the wrapped garments, and hurried into the building with Will by my side. "Harlow! What is your plan? It's not like she's going to be killing this lady as we walk in."

I didn't have a plan so I didn't answer him.

We careened into the lobby. Too impatient for the elevator, I took the stairs, two at a time, Will still right behind me.

At the top, I plowed through the stairwell door, stopping for the briefest second to orient myself. When I'd come here the first time, I'd entered from the parking lot on the *other* side of the building, which meant I'd taken a different set of stairs, I realized. Instead of turning left, like I had before, I turned right. Seconds later, we took a hard turn at the corner. I stopped short and my heart dropped to my stomach at the scene before us. Two paramedics wheeled a gurney toward the other end of the hallway. Abby trailed in its wake.

"Hey!" I hollered, running again. "Abby! What happened?!"

She stopped as the EMTs wheeled the gurney into the elevator. Instead of entering with them, Abby said something to them. The door closed, taking them down. Abby turned to wait for us, pressing the elevator button to call it back. Her face was pale, her eyes red-rimmed. "What happened?" I asked again when I reached her.

"Mrs. Sandoval. She's unresponsive." She dragged the back of her hand under her nose. She glanced at the bundle in my arms, then up at my face, surprised. "You made her the outfit?"

I nodded, feeling the weight of tears filling my eyes. "Is she...?"

"She didn't make it," she croaked. "I'm meeting the ambulance at the hospital."

A belt looped and looped and looped around my insides, tying them into knots. We were too late. The elevator dinged. The doors slid open and without another word, Abby stepped on, leaving us staring at her as the doors closed again and the lift jerked into motion.

My mind spun. We'd been too late. How could she be gone? "I have to see her," I told Will, and I took off for the stairwell.

Less than thirty seconds later, we careened down the other set of stairs, through the lobby, and out the automatic doors into the parking lot. Abby was already in her car, backing out of her parking space. One of the paramedics was climbing into the driver's seat of the ambulance, and the other was closing the back doors of the vehicle, shutting himself inside with Mrs. Sandoval's body.

Rohypnol isn't fatal. Ketamine isn't fatal. Those words shot into my head, ricocheting around like a violent pinball. "The drugs themselves aren't fatal," I said with a hiss, and then I took off running toward the ambulance, Will right next to me, his boots pounding the pavement.

The driver had put the ambulance in gear and was starting to pull out. No sirens. No flashing lights. Because there wasn't anybody to save. Nobody to rush to the hospital.

But no. She *had t*o be alive, just like Jaclyn was alive when she was wheeled into the ambulance. She *had* to be. If there was even a smidgeon of a chance...

A split second and her breathing, that's all I needed... because maybe Mrs. Sandoval's wish would be to simply live. If I could get the garments I'd made for her into the back of the ambulance. If I could let her touch the fabric. Maybe the seams I'd sewn her wishes and dreams into would...

I shoved the handles of the gift bag onto one arm and just as the ambulance started a slow crawl through the parking lot, I launched myself forward and grabbed ahold of the back handle. It was recessed into the door, but I managed to grab ahold of it and yank it down, releasing the locking mechanism. The vehicle jolted to a stop and the back door I held onto swung open. The force of it wrenched my grip free, but Will was right behind me. His hands found my back and he kept me upright, then in one leap, he launched himself past me and into the back. He thrust his arm out, holding my forearm tight, heaving me up and into the ambulance. The paramedic had his back to us. "What the hell, Ospry? Why'd you stop?" He hollered to the driver, clearly thinking it was her bounding in. He didn't turn, though, instead staying focused on Mrs. Sandoval who lay strapped to the gurney.

The tiniest fragment of hope opened up inside of me. If she was already gone like Abby said, he wouldn't be trying to save her. I crouched and stumbled closer, gripping the end of the gurney for balance. I freed the garments from the bag. As I tossed them onto the still body, the tissue paper tore off. At the same moment, the EMT whirled around, gaping at us. It wasn't his face I was looking at, though, it was his hand. The one gloved and pinching Mrs. Sandoval's nostrils closed and pressed down over her closed mouth.

Her body suddenly convulsed, searching for air. "Will!" I screamed.

Will was already in action. He hurled himself past me, landing squarely on Miles Fenton. The sudden impact ripped his hand from Mrs. Sandoval's face. Her mouth opened. Dragged in air. I crawled my way to her, taking her hands.

Will wrestled Miles Fenton, the grunts and groans moving away from me as Will wrenched him out of the ambulance and onto the pavement. The other EMT—Renee Ospry— stared, gaping. Lunging for me like I was the one trying to hurt Yolanda Sandoval. "What are you doing—"

I cut her off. "Oxygen!" I bellowed. "She needs oxygen!"

Ospry seemed to take in the entire scene before her. Will, behind Fenton, restraining him in a chokehold and hollering to some people passing by to call 911. The sunflower blouse and pumpkin pants splayed across Mrs. Sandoval's body. Me clutching her hands. Mrs. Sandoval's ragged efforts to breathe.

Ospry looked at me and I implored her desperately. "Please," I said.

I saw the moment Ospry made a decision. She zigzagged around Will and Fenton, hurling herself into the back of the ambulance. Two vital seconds later, a nasal cannula pushed a steady flow of oxygen into Yolanda Sandoval's nostrils through a length of clear tubing, and a long few seconds after that, the elderly woman's breathing slowed. Steadied. Her entire body relaxed.

I still couldn't believe what I'd seen. Miles Fenton had been suffocating Mrs. Sandoval just as he'd surely done to Jaclyn Padeski while Renee Ospry drove, none the wiser. Just like he'd probably done to Maxine Watson when Abby called 911, sure her accomplice boyfriend was on shift and would be the one dispatched. Maxine Watson had cancer. Her death didn't raise alarms to anyone except Carrie Templeton, and Abby and Fenton had somehow taken care of that. Maybe they'd cut the brake lines, but my research had revealed that that particular scenario, while popular in old TV shows, didn't work quite the way it was portrayed. Carrie Templeton wouldn't have been able to make it all the way up the cliff without knowing that her brakes were not working. Presumably, her car was modern, so the front and rear brake systems might have had independent circuits.

No, the more likely scenario, I realized, was that either Abby or Fenton—or maybe both—had chased Carrie Templeton. Had followed her, aggressively maneuvering her off the cliff. That's why she hadn't braked hard enough or spun out. They'd forced her off the road.

All this passed through my mind in quick, fragmented thoughts. In the distance, the wail of sirens filled the October air. I held one of Mrs. Sandoval's bony hands, her crepey skin loose under my touch. "You're going to be okay," I whispered to her.

Her chest rose and fell.

And then her fingers moved, squeezing mine so lightly it was like a feather dusting against my skin. I caught Ospry's glassy eyes as they shifted to look at Mrs. Sandoval's other hand. A charge of electricity surged through me leaving goose-bumps behind. Because the old woman's arthritic fingers curled around the garments I'd made for her. The fabric bunched in her light grip. The spot at my temple where the silvery roots of hair sprouted tingled. My charm was working right now. Right this very minute. And it was going to save Yolanda Sandoval's life.

Chapter Twenty-Six

The minute hand on the wall clock audibly clicked, marking time. The timepiece had hung in that exact spot, just to the right of the refrigerator, since I could remember. The black cat had a wide smile, a white bowtie, and big eyes that flicked back and forth, right alongside its tail. It should have stopped working years ago. Decades, even, but improbably, it still ticked along.

As the minute hand moved to the twelve, the hour hand on the six, I dropped my embroidery hoop. "Time to get dressed!" I called to Earl Grey as I hurried upstairs and donned my Wednesday Addams costume for the third time, letting her aura settle over me. The Wednesday state of mind was sullen and cheerless, which was the opposite of my natural way of being. And the opposite of how I felt at the moment. Yolanda Sandoval was doing well. She was talking again. Moving around on her own. She was alive.

I would reprise the Wednesday role again, though...for the children.

As I walked downstairs, the doorbell rang. It was still light outside, but when I opened the door, two kids dressed up in their Halloween costumes stared up at me. One of them—the tallest of the three—pointed and said, "Wednesday!"

I nodded morosely. "Very good. Now you'd better leave before Uncle Fester arrives," I deadpanned as I dropped candy into each of their bags. They scurried back down the porch steps, throwing backward nervous glances at me.

A minute later, another knock came on the door. I opened it, this time to a group of three toddlers. They screamed, "Trick or treat!" and held out the orange plastic pumpkins they were using to collect candy.

"Oh my goodness!" I exclaimed, not bothering to stay in Wednesday's character for them. They were too little to know the difference. "You are the most adorable gnomes I have ever seen!"

It was true. They all had pointy hats, long beards, long shirts, and oversized felt-shaped boots to cover their shoes. The littlest gave a toothless grin from under her flowing whiskers. "Tank you!"

I couldn't help but chuckle with delight. They were precious. "Are you sisters?" I asked, dropping a miniature candy bar into each plastic pumpkin.

"Mmm-hmm," the middle one said with a nod that dislodged her hat. "Oh!"

"Oh!" I straightened it and told them to wait, left them at the door, and ran into my atelier. I returned with a handful of bobby pins, quickly using them to strengthen the attachment between the gnome hat and the beard.

"Come on," the tallest of the three said, pulling on the littlest's arm. "Tank you!" the littlest girl said again, then the other two echoed her with, "Thank you! Thank you!" as they scurried back down the porch steps, over the flagstone path, and out to the sidewalk where their parents waited.

Another group traipsed up, these kids heading firmly into their teen years. "Trick or treat," they muttered, their enthusiasm at least fifty degrees less than the gnomes who'd come before them. One of them looked mildly impressed with my Wednesday outfit, but not enough to muster a full smile.

The four kids who came next were a little bit older, still, and one of their voices cracked in the way puberty caused. I looked at them in pure stony-faced Wednesday style and in the emptiest voice I could, said, "What kind of dystopian hellscape is this?"

They looked at each other, then back at me. The boy with the squeaky voice—who, like all of the others, had put minimal effort into his costume, wearing normal jeans and a t-shirt with a scary mask—cleared his throat. "Who are you supposed to be?" he said, this time his words clear and with no pubescent squeak.

His friend backhanded him. "Dude. Come one. It's Wednesday. You know, The Addams Family."

"You boys best be moving along," I said dryly, "but if you stay, it'll just be some light torture, and don't worry, I won't leave a mark."

They stared at me through their masks. "Huh?" one of them said.

"It's a quote?" I said. "It's what Wednesday says in the last episode."

"If you say so," the squeaky-voiced boy said, and he held his pillowcase out.

"You're too old to trick or treat," I said, hands on hips, but they stood firm so I dropped a single mini candy into each of their monstrously big bags. I felt sorry for their teachers tomorrow. If I could minimize their sugar high even by a single Snickers Bar, then I would.

They grumbled, from my stinginess, I guessed, and trudged down the porch steps without a single thank you.

I needed more adorable gnomes in my life.

Will turned up thirty minutes later, sans his Xavier

costume. "Late meeting," he said after a lovely kiss hello. He gestured to my black dress and Wednesday wig. "I weighed my options. Go home to change, or come straight here to see you." He grinned and whispered in my ear. "I chose to come here."

I tamped down my smile and leveled my gaze at him, once again adopting my monotone Wednesday persona, and deadpanned another quote from the TV show. "For some reason I cannot fathom or indulge, you seem to like me."

He cracked a crooked smile and waggled his brows, then tapped his fingers as if he were counting. "Oh, I can fathom many reasons to like you," he said. "You're brilliant. You're beautiful. You're clever—"

He kissed me again just as the doorbell rang, but he let his lips linger, his hands on my hips, my own arms draped over his shoulders. For a few seconds, the rest of the world disappeared. That's what Will Flores did to me. "I can fathom plenty of reasons to like you, too," I said.

The doorbell rang and rang, like someone was pressing it down and decided to leave their finger there.

"Okay, okay!" I said, finally breaking away from Will. I flung open the door expecting more littles trick-or-treating. Instead, it was Nana, Mama, and Hoss McClaine. Nana wore a shepherd's dress and bonnet, holding a crook in her right hand. "Little Bo Peep lost her sheep," I said, still keeping my monotone Wednesday tone. "You lose your goats."

"Baaahhh," she said with a dismissive wave of her hand. "That doesn't rhyme, now, does it? Creative license."

Mama was a bumble bee, complete with a faux stinger, and Hoss had bright flower petals around his face and wore all green. "Adorable," I said, meaning it. Hoss grimaced, but the glint in his eyes told me he'd play whatever games Tessa Cassidy had in store for him. I had to laugh at how they'd stayed true to their charms with their costumes.

Orphie and Gavin showed up next, without trick-or-treat bags or costumes. We moved to the front porch where I'd dragged the kitchen chairs out, knowing I wouldn't be alone that night. Orphie and I took the rocking chairs. Mama perched on Hoss's lap where he had one arm around her hips and the other resting lightly on her knee. Their newlywed phase might well last a lifetime, I thought.

Will and Gavin leaned against the porch railing, while Nana sat on the lip of one of the ladder-backed chairs, leaning forward and grasping her crook like a cane. She looked ready to pounce at the first sight of Thelma Louise on the loose.

"They confessed," Gavin announced once the trick-or-treaters had trickled down to few and far between.

I knew he was talking about Abby Lassiter and Miles Fenton and, instantly, I felt as if the weight of the world had been lifted from my shoulders. "Why'd they do it?"

He answered my question with his own. "Why do people murder?"

I'd seen enough to know the broad answer to that. "Greed. Jealousy. Revenge. Hatred. Or maybe they're backed into a corner, so self-preservation."

He nodded like he agreed with my response. "In this case, it was pure greed. Abby Lassiter saw the opportunity to take from the elderly. A necklace here. An antique there. She figured no one would miss it. Those two have done this before. Like Bonnie and Clyde. We went through the hospital records of incoming patients by ambulance, focusing on Miles Fenton. More than fifty percent came in deceased. Abby had been a caregiver for *all* of them. They spread it out over a few years. The people were elderly—often with no family to speak of—so no one suspected a thing."

"Until Carrie Templeton," I said.

Gavin nodded. "Until Carrie Templeton. Abby drugged her drink and then got her into her car before it took full effect. She drove Carrie and Miles followed. By the time they got to the cliff, Carrie Templeton was out cold. They just put it in neutral and rolled the car right off the cliff. No brake marks because she wasn't even driving. Then they just drove away."

I hadn't gotten that quite right, but I was close.

"What about that blackmailer?" Nana asked.

Hoss cleared his throat. "As they say, people confess things to their hairdressers. We assume Carrie Templeton told her her suspicions and Jaclyn took over from there."

My phone pinged with an incoming text. I looked at it, tuning out the chatter of the people—*my* people—all around me. It was from Madelyn Brighton.

Thought you might like to see these.

A series of photos appeared, all of them of Juletta in my kitchen. They were from the day Meemaw had displaced her, taking over her body. I gasped as I registered the shimmery aura of light hugging the shape of Juletta's body, but it was the last photo that stunned me the most. A vaporous cloud hovered above the ground a few feet from Juletta. I remembered that moment. Juletta's body had jerked and a misty form had stepped right out of her, jolting her in the process. Madelyn had captured the seconds after that when Will and I had been focused on making sure Juletta was okay.

The glimmering vortex, frozen by the photograph, flared as bright as the full moon in the Halloween sky. Meemaw.

My gasp made all eyes turn to me. "Okay, darlin'?" Mama asked, head tilted curiously.

The porch lights suddenly flickered, and then the garden lights illuminated the flowers Mama kept in bloom. "Fine," I said, smiling.

The gate at the sidewalk creaked open and Gracie, Libby, and Holly appeared in their same costumes. They walked up the flagstone path, arm in arm. Behind them the gate swung closed.

Gracie glanced over her shoulder, then caught my eye. She grinned. "Loretta Mae?" and my smile grew, and the lights flickered some more.

Holly's eyes grew wide as she looked around. "Sometimes this place feels like it's haunted," she said.

Gracie and Libby doubled over laughing. Gavin's cheeks had turned ruddy and he looked shaken. He knew the rumors. Hoss knew the truth. Gavin just didn't want to believe it, but I knew he did. And I trusted him to keep the Cassidy secret.

"You don't know the half of it, Holly," I said. "And you behave, Meemaw," I muttered under my breath. Orphie shot me a look and I winked at her. I felt a warm breath on my cheek, the soft flutter of something against my arm. As my rocking chair started moving, I sent a quick thank you text to Madelyn then closed my phone and put it down. I didn't need to look at the photos right now to see Meemaw because she was right here next to me, and I had almost all the Cassidy women, all charmed because of Butch himself, here with me, too.

"Happy Halloween, Meemaw," I whispered. In the yard, the leaves of the pecan tree rustled in response.

THE END

Read more by Melissa Bourbon

Read the Entire Series

GET THEM HERE!

Pleating for Mercy

A Fitting End

Deadly Patterns

A Custom-Fit Crime

A Killing Notion

A Seamless Murder

Get more Harlow, Meemaw, and the whole Bliss gang!

About Melissa Bourbon

Melissa Bourbon is the national bestselling author of more than 35 mystery books, including the Lola Cruz Mysteries, A Magical Dressmaking Mystery series, the Bread Shop Mysteries, written as Winnie Archer, and the Book Magic Mysteries. She is also the founder of WriterSpark Academy & Book Cover Design.

Melissa lives in North Carolina with her educator husband, Carlos. She is beyond fortunate to be living the life of her dreams.

VISIT Melissa's website at http://www.melissabourbon.com

JOIN her online book club at https://www.facebook.com/groups/BookWarriors/

JOIN her book review club at https://facebook.com/melissaanddianesreviewclub

Books by Melissa

Book Magic Mysteries
The Secret on Rum Runner's Lane
Murder in Devil's Cove
Murder at Sea Captain's Inn
Murder Through an Open Door
Murder and an Irish Curse

Lola Cruz Mysteries
Living the Vida Lola
Hasta la Vista, Lola!
Bare-Naked Lola
What Lola Wants
Drop Dead Lola

Bread Shop Mysteries, *written as Winnie Archer*
Kneaded to Death
Crust No One
The Walking Bread
Flour in the Attic
Dough or Die
Death Gone a-Rye
A Murder Yule Regret
Bread Over Troubled Water

Magical Dressmaking Mysteries

Pleating for Mercy

A Fitting End

Deadly Patterns

A Custom-Fit Crime

A Killing Notion

A Seamless Murder

Bobbin for Answers

Bodice of Evidence

Mystery/Suspense

Silent Obsession

Silent Echoes

Deadly Legends Boxed Set

Paranormal Romance

Storiebook Charm

Printed in Great Britain
by Amazon